The Sword and the Spirit

Book Two

~ GABRIEL ~

Avril Borthiry

Note: Dates used are taken from the Julian calendar, which was in use at the time.

'Finally, brothers, whatever is true, whatever is honourable, whatever is just, whatever is pure, whatever is lovely, whatever is commendable, if there is any excellence, if there is anything worthy of praise, think about these things.'

Philippians 4:8

Chapter One

Castle Cathan
The western Highlands of Scotland
Tuesday the 9th day of May, year of the Lord 1308.

"I would have preferred a quiet departure." Gabriel threw a scowl at the stable door as he settled the saddle on Kadar's broad back. "There must be twenty people out there."

"Twenty-six." Ewan gave a sober smile. "Cannae be helped, Brother. For some unfathomable reason, folks here have grown fond of you and willnae let you sneak away under cover of darkness."

"I am *not* sneaking away." Still scowling, Gabriel tugged the girth tight and fastened it. "My decision to depart has never been a secret, but I would prefer *not* to have a congregation observing the event. Which begs the question of who told them I intended to leave this morning."

"I couldnae say." Ewan cleared his throat. "But you ken we all wish you'd reconsider the leaving part."

Gabriel squirmed inwardly. "We've discussed this a dozen times, Ewan. You know my reasons."

"Aye, I know your reasons." Ewan shrugged. "Doesnae mean I have to agree with them, especially since the falsehoods spoken about our order have now polluted English ears. The persecution is no longer limited to France, Gabriel. Templars are being arrested in England too."

"Few and far between, if our sources are correct."

"That may be so, but why take the risk? I'm telling you, leaving Scotland at this time is a mistake. You should wait a while longer and see what comes of all this." Ewan grimaced. "Though it'll be nothing good, I warrant."

"The risk is small." Gabriel frowned as he fastened his saddle bags to the back of the saddle. "Besides, I'll be surrendering the mantle once I reach the abbey."

"Another mistake," Ewan muttered, after a moment of telling silence.

Hackles bristling, Gabriel cast a challenging glare at his friend. "Devoting my life to God is a *mistake*?"

Ewan heaved a sigh and ran a hand through his hair. "Dinnae twist my words, Brother. 'Tis no' the taking up of the cloth which bothers me. 'Tis the laying down of your sword. You're a knight as much as you are a monk. I admire your intent to devote your life to the church, but I question the wisdom of it. I also question the *why* of it."

The words poked at a weak spot in Gabriel's resolve, as was undoubtedly Ewan's intent. Gabriel regarded the man for a moment— a man who knew him better than anyone—a man he'd come to love as a blood brother, let alone a brother-in-arms.

Like Gabriel, Ewan MacKellar had devoted much of his life to the Templar order. He was a fine warrior, with an honourable heart—and a streak of Scottish stubbornness a mile wide. For the past six months, Ewan's Highland home had served as a sanctuary for Gabriel and Jacques, ever since the three of them, plus a young squire, had escaped the mass arrest of the Templars in France.

"Castle Cathan is your home, Ewan," Gabriel said, at last. "'Tis where you belong. You surrendered your mantle willingly, certain of where your heart lay. You now have a wife and will soon have a child. You are, for want of a better word, reconciled."

A brief frown flitted across Ewan's brow. "And you are not."

"Nay." Gabriel bent to retrieve his shield, moved to Kadar's head, and took hold of the reins. "I'm still a Templar, sworn to fight in God's name. 'Tis the only life I've known for the past ten years. I had faith in its continuance, but now it's all crumbling to dust. In truth, I'm not certain that monastic life is what I seek. Christ knows, I'm not certain of anything except that I cannot stay here, wondering and waiting. I have to leave. I have to explore different paths, and trust that God will guide me onto the right one. If nothing else, my time at Furness will allow me to reflect."

"I understand." Ewan grimaced and scratched his head. "Well, somewhat. Though we do have abbeys in Scotland too. Could you no' do your reflecting on the right side of the border?"

Gabriel's mouth twitched. "As your sister so frequently reminds me, I'm a *Sasunnach* from the wrong side of the border. And besides, Father Simon—"

"Is a friend. Aye, I ken." Ewan heaved a sigh and placed a hand on Gabriel's shoulder. "Well, God knows I'll miss you, Brother, for many reasons. But mostly because I'll have no one to taunt."

Gabriel allowed himself a smile. "Your taunting never bothered me in the least. I just let you believe it did."

Ewan's grin failed to offset a visible glint of moisture in his eyes. "Bollocks," he said, his voice wavering. "You took the bait every time."

The gloom in the stable deepened as Jacques appeared at the doorway, his pale mantle declaring his identity and his creed. "Did you manage to change his mind, Ewan?" he asked.

Ewan gave Gabriel's shoulder a squeeze and then released it. "Nay."

Jacques heaved a sigh. "May I try again?"

"Nay," Gabriel replied. "You may not." He clicked his tongue and tugged on Kadar's reins. "Step aside, Brothers. I have to go."

Before you do *manage to change my mind.*

With Kadar in tow, Gabriel stepped out into the courtyard, where a chilly west wind skipped over the castle walls and tugged at his mantle… and where a crowd had gathered beneath paling dawn skies to bid him farewell.

"God help me," he muttered, disquieted by the sentiment that hung in the air like an invisible fog, one utterly immune to the sea breeze. He tugged the reins over Kadar's head, and reached for the saddle, meaning to mount up. But, as if stayed by an invisible hand, he paused and drew breath.

By virtue of his birth alone, Gabriel was an enemy to these people. Yet they had welcomed him into their lives and treated him as one of their own. Without question. Oh, he'd made his gratitude known over the past few days—polite declarations of thanks, scattered here and there like dry crumbs. It had been all he could manage.

Sharing the contents of his heart with God came easily to Gabriel. Putting his thoughts down on parchment also gave him little trouble. But expressing his inner feelings to mortal souls had always been a challenge, one he tended to avoid.

He became aware of Ewan's approach.

"You cannae just ride away without a word, Brother," he murmured, voicing Gabriel's exact thought. "You owe them more than that."

"I know I do." Gabriel turned, first to Ewan, and then to those gathered around. He drew another breath and gave some power to his voice. "I owe all of you more than I can ever repay. For what it's worth, your kindness to me will never be forgotten."

"We'll miss you, Gabriel," Morag, Ewan's sister, announced, "though, I swear by all things holy, I cannae believe I'm saying that to a Sasunnach." Ripples of laughter followed, though they had no real substance.

Cristie stepped forward. "Your kindness to me will never be forgotten either, Gabriel," she said. "May God bless you and keep you safe."

"And you, my lady." He regarded Ewan's young wife with genuine fondness, casting a glance at the slight rise of her belly. "I shall look forward to hearing news of your child's birth."

Cristie moved her hand to where her child lay. "We'll let you know, of course."

Gabriel then shifted his gaze to Hammett— the young squire who had fled with them from France. "Hammett," he said, with some sternness, and the lad straightened his spine.

"Aye, Master?"

"Take care of my brothers."

A glint of pride came to Hammett's eyes, and he straightened a little more. "I will, Master."

Gabriel nodded his approval and glanced about, daring to embrace his final few moments at this remote Scottish outpost.

The solid curtain walls had been built to keep invaders at bay, but the wind forever mocked them, cresting the battlements to swoop and swirl unchallenged around those who dwelt within. The muffled thunder of waves crashed eternally upon the shore, while above, a cacophony of sea birds filled the air from morn till eve. Such was the music of Castle Cathan.

And I will miss it.

"Right, well, I think that's enough." The voice— that of Ruaidri MacKellar, laird of Castle Cathan— pulled Gabriel from his reflections. "I think we should let this poor man be on his way. Open the gates."

Supressing a sigh, Gabriel hoisted himself into the saddle and looked down at Ewan's elder brother. "I appreciate all you have done for our order, Laird MacKellar," he said, "and all you continue to do."

"'Tis my honour to do it," Ruaidri replied. "The Bruce himself has made it clear that the Templars are welcome in Scotland. Castle Cathan will always be open to those who need shelter. That said, do you have the letter of safe conduct? There are some of us, I fear, who might see you as a *Sasunnach* rather than a Templar."

Gabriel gathered up the reins. "Aye, I have it."

Ruaidri nodded. "Good."

"He also has his sword," Ewan murmured. "I pity the poor bastard who dares to challenge that."

Jacques placed a hand on Gabriel's boot and looked up at him, his clenched jaw suggesting suppressed emotion. "I pray neither the letter nor your sword will be needed, Brother. Send us news of your safe arrival, and may you find the peace you seek."

"And if you ever feel the need to return…" Tears shone in Ewan's eyes as he cleared his throat. "Dinnae think twice. Despite what you said, this is your home as much as it is mine. And it will always be."

Gabriel's gut tightened. Maybe he should have kept his departure secret after all and sneaked away under cover of darkness. At least he wouldn't have had to face this merciless onslaught of sentiment.

"I find myself without words," he said. "At least, none that will do justice to what lies in my heart at this moment. I'm blessed to call you friend. Each and every one of you. 'Tis all I can think of to say."

"More than enough." Ruaidri stepped back and gestured toward the open gates. "Be on your way, Templar. And may God go with you."

Chapter Two

Eight days later.
Church of St. Bega, Cumberland, England.

It was the shallow end of night. Soon, the cock would crow and the church-bell would rouse folks from their beds, but for now, the land rested in silence. Breanna cast a glance at the sky as she placed her hand on the iron latch.

"Wait here, Theo," she whispered to her escort, who stood beside her on the church steps, "I'll not be long."

She lifted the latch and pushed. The hefty door swung open with a groan as if complaining at the ungodly hour. Breanna, clutching her basket, stepped into the dark interior and let the door close behind her with a repeated groan that echoed wearily off the walls. Inhaling the musty odour of tallow and incense, she dipped her fingers in the small font and crossed herself before moving toward the altar, where a solitary candleflame burnt a hole in the darkness. She crossed herself once more as she tiptoed past it and approached a small, arched doorway that sat flush in the wall. As she moved to set the basket down, the door swung open, and a shadowy figure emerged, a flickering taper clutched in one hand.

Breanna stifled a squeal. "Father Dunstan! By all the saints, you startled me."

"Breanna! What are you doing here?" the priest demanded in a voice worn down to a croak. He rubbed at one eye and regarded the basket. "What is this?"

"I awoke early and felt like going for a walk." Breanna, still catching her breath, held the basket out. "Walter told me you were poorly, Father, so I've brought some honey for your throat, and ginger and mint for a tisane. I'm sorry if I woke you. How are you feeling?"

"I wasn't asleep, and 'tis but a mild ague that plagues me. Nothing serious." Frowning, he took the basket and looked past her into the belly of the church. "My thanks, child. Who escorted you?"

"Um, no one."

The priest made a sound of disapproval. "By all the saints, Breanna. You know you should not be out alone at this hour. Or at any hour, in truth."

"Well, I'm not exactly alone," she countered, failing to prevent a flare of heat from colouring her cheeks. "I met Theo on the way here. He's waiting outside."

The priest gave her a reproving look. "Theo would be of little use in the event of any trouble."

Breanna patted the dagger at her belt. "I have this, too."

"And Heaven forbid you be obliged to use it. I assume your uncle is unaware you are here?"

Breanna fidgeted. "He was still abed when I left."

"I see." Father Dunstan's chest rattled as he drew a sigh. He looked down at the basket for a moment and then regarded her once more, his expression softer. "'Twas a kind thought, my dear, but you should never venture out without an armed escort. Those who live outside the law have been increasingly brazen of late. These are dangerous times."

Breanna sighed too. "And I'm weary of being a martyr to them, Father. Every portal at Ghyllhead is guarded. 'Tis like a prison."

"For your own protection, as well as that of everyone else within. Which also begs the question of how you managed to elude those guards."

"I did not elude them." She lifted her chin. "I told Alfred where I was going."

"And charmed the witless fool into letting you pass, no doubt, when he should have come with you." Father Dunstan's chest rattled again. "Truly, Breanna, my poorly throat does not merit the risk you've taken. Let me freshen myself and sound the morning bell, then I'll escort you back to Ghyllhead."

Breanna shook her head. "Oh, nay, Father, I've no wish to trouble you. You should rest. 'Tis but a short walk, and I know how to use my dagger and in Theo's defence, I believe you underestimate his worth. I'm sure I'll be—"

"Some fresh morning air will do me no harm." He raised a brow and gestured toward the interior of the church. "Might I suggest you spend some time reflecting on the folly of your actions while you wait? I'll return momentarily."

Breanna opened her mouth to argue, but Father Dunstan's raised brow deterred her. "Very well, but can Theo come in and wait with me?"

"Of course." He gave her a wry smile. "I know how much he appreciates the sanctity of this place."

Breanna returned the smile, though a measure of guilt weighed on her conscience as she made her way back to the main door. Her pre-dawn flight from the confines of Ghyllhead had, at first, felt like an accomplishment. An act of defiance against those whose actions caused others to live in fear. But Father Dunstan's reprimand, while gentle, had merit. Her uncle would not be pleased, and rightly so.

Worse, he'll be disappointed.

The heat of shame once again arose in her cheeks as she pulled the door open.

"Theo, you can—" Puzzled by the empty step, she glanced about. The sky showed signs of paling, yet shadows of night remained, thick and black. "Theo?"

As Breanna lifted her skirts and descended the church step, one of the shadows came to life and moved toward her—a man, undoubtedly, his silhouette a solid layer of blackness against the receding night.

Breanna let out a squeal as a rush of fear, like an icy wave, enveloped her. "You frightened me, sir," she said, startling herself with the involuntary spill of her words. As he drew near, she realized the man's face lay hidden behind a helm—a cylinder of pockmarked steel that amplified the ominous hiss of his breath. Only the dirty whites of his eyes, like pallid splinters, could be seen through the visor slits. As he regarded her, those same splinters widened briefly before narrowing again. Head tilted as if appraising her, he half-drew the sword that rested against his hip. And the reason for his presence, terrifying in its reality, crashed into Breanna's unprepared mind.

Clearly, the man was not there to make his confession. Nor had he expected to be confronted by anyone other than a defenceless priest. Certainly not a woman, and especially a woman like Breanna.

Dear God. I should not have spoken.

But even if she had not said a word, her appearance declared her status. Her fur-trimmed cloak with its silver pin, the garnet ring on her right hand, her wealth of brown curls, brushed and braided—all of these things identified her as a high-born female, worth far more than a brass chalice and paten, or a few paltry coins from the alms pouch.

To this renegade—for he could surely be nothing else—she was an unforeseen bounty, and he'd already recognized her value. As she opened her mouth to scream, his free arm struck out like a snake, closed around her neck, and pulled her hard into his chest.

"If you want to live, my lady," he growled, his voice sounding hollow inside the helmet, "you'll stay quiet."

Face pressed into the coarse wool of his tunic, Breanna struggled to take air as she groped for her dagger. "Please, I ca-can't breathe."

"Then cease your struggling." His hand crushed her fingers as they wrapped around the hilt of her blade. "And don't be foolish."

She yelped as he twisted her wrist, the pain forcing her to release the dagger, which clattered onto the steps. Then he grabbed a handful of her hair, jerked her head back, and bent his face to hers, foul breath leaching through the perforations in his helmet. "And be *quiet*."

"Breanna?" Father Dunstan's voice rang out from the depths of the church. "Is everything all right?"

Trembling, Breanna gazed into her captor's shrouded eyes. "Don't hurt him," she whispered, "please."

"Then do as I say," the man growled, dragging her down the steps, "and he'll not be harmed."

Another man stepped out of the shadows, his face also shielded by steel. "What's this? What've ye found?" He then gasped, audibly. "Sweet Mother of Christ, is that—?"

"Bite your tongue," her captor snarled, sheathing his sword. "Tell the others to set the fires quickly and get out. It seems we've already got more than we came for, so I'm leaving now before the alarm is raised. 'Tis too rich a prize to risk losing. Nothing else has changed, so keep to the agreed route. You know where to find me." His hot breath escaped the helmet and brushed across Breanna's scalp. "And kill the priest if he puts up a fight."

"Nay!" Breanna struggled against him. "You said—"

"I said, be *quiet*." A large, callused hand landed hard across her mouth, forcing her teeth into her bottom lip. She tasted blood and felt the burn of tears. The man's iron-like grip held her fast as he hauled her around the side of the church into a stand of trees, where several horses stood in tethered silence.

Breanna fought to keep her wits about her, but fear robbed her of the ability to focus. Her legs felt boneless, bile scorched back of her throat, and her heart pounded so hard it hurt. And what of Theo? She took some comfort from the fact that she'd seen no sign of him at all. When the men had first appeared, he'd likely bolted for the woods, unseen and unheard. Such was his way.

But other questions whirled through her mind like snowflakes in a north wind.

Who are these men? Have they killed Father Dunstan? Protect him, God, please. Where is he taking me? Will I be harmed? Will I be killed?

Her captor's words came back to her.

'Too rich a prize to risk losing'.

A small voice of reason spoke up. Nay, she would not be killed. At least, not unless their ransom demand wasn't met. And that thought made her even more dizzy with despair, though not for herself, but for her uncle. What price would her foolishness cost him? And not just him, but those who relied on him?

Breanna closed her eyes. *I'm so sorry, Uncle.*

"Now, my lady." Her captor halted by one of the horses. "We can do this painlessly or we can do it your way. Makes no difference to me."

He kept a tight hold on her, but removed his hand from her mouth.

Without hesitation, Breanna turned her head and spat bloodied spittle at the visor-slits in the man's helmet. He flinched, visibly.

"May the Devil take you and yours," Breanna said,

her voice trembling.

The man raised a clenched fist and muttered something under his breath. Breanna struggled to keep her knees from buckling and kept her defiant gaze fixed on him as she waited for the blow. It never came. Instead, he dropped the fist and thrust Breanna, belly-first, against the horse's flank.

"Very well." He pinned her in place with his body as he reached into a saddlebag. "We'll do it your way."

She pushed against him, to no avail. "May you rot in Hell, you—"

The rest of Breanna's curse remained unsaid, interrupted by a filthy gag forced between her teeth and tied tightly at the back of her head. The foul taste made her stomach heave, and fresh tears sprang to her eyes. Her captor clucked his tongue.

"Have a care not to spew," he muttered. "'Twould be a pity to see you choke to death. Dead, you're worth nothing."

A flare of hate supplanted Breanna's fear. She gave a muffled cry and struggled against man and horse. The horse snorted his displeasure but didn't move.

"Have a care, lass." The man ground his pelvis against the base of her spine, his hardened state quite obvious. "You're arousing me."

Breanna froze.

Chuckling, her captor's gloved hands slid around to her stomach, pulled her wrists together, and bound them tightly. Then he turned her to face him.

"I'll take that," he said, tugging the ring from her

finger, ignoring another muffled cry of protest. The ring had little intrinsic value, but it had belonged to Breanna's mother. Sentimentally, it was priceless. "And if you anger me again, I'll remove the finger as well, and send it along with the ransom demand."

Still obviously aroused, he pressed himself against her, the echo of his breath heavy and hard within the confines of his helm. "You're a pretty little thing," he muttered, dragging a hand over her breast and squeezing. "Very tempting."

Fighting tears, Breanna lifted her chin and dared to keep her gaze locked with his. He chuckled again and hoisted her into the saddle like a trussed animal. Then he clambered up behind and pulled her against him.

Fear thrummed in Breanna's ears like the low buzz of a fly, yet in some untouched part of her brain, she remained oddly aware of other sounds. A blackbird shouted out his morning refrain from a thicket. A horse nearby shook his head and gave a low whinny. And from somewhere in the distance came the terrified scream of a woman.

Breanna looked toward the village, though the corner of the church blocked her view of it. She whimpered and prayed she only imagined a dancing flicker of light that disturbed the receding darkness.

'...set the fires, and get out.'

Then another scream drifted out of the silence, followed by shouts and cries of men. Breanna threw a desperate glance toward the castle. Surely, they must have noticed the attack by now.

Alfred, Elwyn, please. Sound the alarm.

As if in response, a torch flared bright above the battlements. Then another, and another. Breanna could not hear the watchmen's call to arms, but she knew they'd given it. Her captor knew it too.

"I believe you've seen enough, my lady," he said, and her world went dark as he settled a blindfold over her eyes. "'Tis time to go."

Breanna's choked cry of protest had no means of escape. The hiss of her captor's breath heightened as he gathered up the reins, wheeled his horse around, and spurred it into a canter.

Blind and helpless, Breanna was shaken like a cloth doll as they rode. Never in her worst nightmares had she felt such fear. She gripped the pommel as well as she could with her bound hands, but if not for the man's arms holding her in place, she'd have been thrown from the saddle several times. Fighting against nausea and an urge to piss, she endeavoured to settle her mind and heart. With no small effort, she forced herself make some sense of her situation, to reason against the terror that threatened to fling her into a well of hysterics.

First, who might have taken her? A man not without some education, she thought, judging by his articulate speech. *And English. Not Scottish.* She pondered. *Or were there hints of Scotland buried in his voice? Accents could be falsified.*

A nobleman who had fallen from grace and taken up outlawry, perhaps? Nay, that seemed improbable. A mercenary knight, then, who exploited opportunity in the chaos of conflict. He would not be the first to do so. English and Scot alike, indifferent to their origins, sought to profit from the misery of others on both sides of the border.

Only a devil without a heart would dare plunder a house of God. And where is he taking me?

Without her sight, Breanna could not be certain of their direction, though she knew it would most likely be northerly and likely by way of lesser-known trails. The frequent twists and turns implied a winding, narrow path. And despite the blindfold, she had perceived fleeting ripples of light and shadow as they travelled, which suggested a forest canopy lay overhead.

A little calmer, Breanna closed her blindfolded eyes and focused on her small beacon of rationale. In doing so, awareness of her physical discomfort grew stronger. The roiling in her stomach had not ceased, and her arse hurt like the devil from all the bouncing around. How long had they been travelling? It felt like forever. The laboured rush of air from the horse's lungs suggested the poor creature had about reached its limit. As had Breanna's bladder. She shifted in the saddle and nudged the man in the ribs.

He ignored her, so she did it again, with more urgency.

His elbows closed inwards like the pincers of a crab, squeezing her arms against her body. "Do that once more, lady, and you'll be sor—"

It happened in a heartbeat—an abrupt, violent lurch, as if they'd hit a wall. Breanna barely had time to realize she'd left the saddle before the impact with the ground drove air from her lungs and buried her face in the damp earth. A light exploded behind her eyes as pain shot through her shoulder and neck. Then something hefty thudded into the earth beside her with a loud snap and a single huff of breath. A moment later came the snort of a horse, a prolonged rattle of harness, and the tell-tale thrum of hooves fading into the distance.

Breanna moved her head, flinching at a sharp stab of pain shooting through her shoulder. Tears flooded her eyes as she tried, and failed, to snatch a breath. Desperate for air, she clawed at the gag with numb fingers, freed her mouth and filled her lungs. Then, chest heaving, she turned onto her back and pushed the blindfold from her eyes. Warm tears escaped over her temples as she blinked up into a canopy of trees and grey skies.

"Dear God," she whispered, closing her eyes for a moment as nausea swamped her. She could not fight it, and turned her head to heave and spit out bile, the motion yet another lesson in agony—and fear.

Her captor lay on his back beside her, head twisted and staring, the whites of his eyes visible through the eye-slits. Breanna held her breath and waited for him to move, to speak. But he did neither, not even when she bit back her pain and sat up. Only then did she see the grotesque angle of the man's neck and recalled the sharp snap she'd heard as he fell. It had not been a twig, she realized, with a shiver of horror.

The man's eyes, though open, saw nothing.

What had happened? She could only surmise the

weary horse had stumbled, catching its distracted rider unawares. Breanna glanced about, hoping the creature might still linger nearby, but saw no sign of it. She wasn't even certain which way it had gone. The forest trail, narrow and unfamiliar, snaked off in both directions, while around her, the woodland stretched away in thick, shadowed silence. A sense of isolation trailed an icy finger down her spine. Lost and alone, her ordeal was not yet over.

Far from it, in truth.

"Move," she murmured, and shifted onto her knees, cringing as another stab of pain pierced her shoulder. Before she could go anywhere, she needed to remove her bonds. Her wrists burned, and her fingers, starved of blood, had turned alarmingly pale. Still on her knees, she shuffled closer to the dead man, dampness from the earth soaking through her skirts.

Despite all he had done, Breanna felt a twinge of compassion for the loss of his sorry life. She considered trying to remove his helm, curious to see his face, but the grotesque angle of his head deterred her. Instead, she offered up a prayer for his soul and leaned over him, looking for his sword.

To her frustration, he appeared to be lying atop it. Only part of the hilt was visible, jutting from beneath his left hip, on the other side and out of her reach. Wincing with pain, Breanna half-crawled and half-shuffled around the body, pondering its identity. All outward appearances—the boots and clothes—gave the impression of a man of some means.

Breanna's gaze fell upon his gloved hands. Perhaps

she should check for a signet ring, a jewel that might identify him. Such information might redeem her in her uncle's eyes. Somewhat, at least. She should also search him for her ring, too,

First, though, she needed to free her bonds. She reached for the sword hilt.

Before she'd even touched it, a sound drifted through the trees, and the hair on her neck lifted. Holding her breath, she looked back along the trail, the way they'd come. And the sound came again.

A man's voice. Nay, *men's* voices. A shout. The whinny of a horse. The runaway horse? Had it caught someone's attention? Whose? A chill brushed the nape of Breanna's neck.

'Keep to the agreed route.'

Could it be them already? On their way to wherever, having completed their cowardly morning foray? If not, then who? No one of good repute, for sure. These woods were haunted by those who lived outside of the law. It would not bode well for Breanna to be discovered alone and defenceless.

"Christ, help me." Gritting her teeth, she tugged on the sword hilt with cold, unfeeling fingers. The thing barely moved, and a fresh lance of pain shot through her shoulder, forcing tears to her eyes. She cast a frantic glance down the winding trail, knowing that whoever approached would, at any moment, come into view. And if she could see them, they could see her.

At that same instant, a flock of crows took flight in unison from a nearby tree, their raucous cries echoing across the sky. It sounded like a warning, a call to action, telling Breanna she had no more time. She had to leave.

Now.

Nothing less than a force of will lifted her to her feet. Yet, even on the edge of panic, she glanced heavenward and chose her direction with aforethought, choosing the darker edge of the sky, where remnants of night yet lingered. West. A direction that would, with God's good grace, take her closer to Ghyllhead, rather than away from it. Biting down against stiffness and pain, she headed straight into the forest, running as fast as her legs—and her skirts—would allow.

With some relief, Breanna found herself in an overgrown realm where a horse would be hard-pressed to travel at any speed. But in her injured and shackled state, that same realm presented her with a similar challenge. Pain accompanied her every step, and her bound hands compromised her ability to balance as she navigated the rough terrain. As for direction, the cloud-ridden skies gave little away, though at that point, Breanna didn't really care. She just needed to put distance between herself and the men.

Chest heaving, she halted and pressed her spine against the trunk of a tree, needing a moment of respite. Her bladder cried out to be emptied, and she squatted down to relieve herself. She had barely finished when from somewhere behind her came a distant shout—a harsh cry that told of a gruesome discovery. They—assuming it was the raiders—had obviously discovered their leader's body. And they would no doubt be looking for her.

Breanna stifled a sob and bolted once more, praying the men would neither see nor hear her flight through the forest. Driven by fear, she dodged trees, stumbled over fallen branches and splashed through mud. As she pushed through a patch of dense undergrowth, her cloak caught on a bramble, halting her mid-stride. Teeth gritted, she tugged at it, which only served to anchor the thorns deeper into the fabric.

"Come on," she whispered, trying to pull herself free. "Please!"

Another shout drifted through the trees. Desperate, Breanna unfastened her cloak, let it fall, and sped onward. Panic invigorated her, giving wings to her feet. The rasp of her breath and the pounding of her heart filled her ears and head. She heard nothing else, and her surroundings became a blur. Time surely passed, but had little meaning.

When fatigue at last returned, it came in a crippling rush and turned her legs to sand. At the point of collapse, Breanna threw a desperate glance over her shoulder, seeing ominous shadows moving like ghosts through the trees, her imagination heightened by exhaustion and fear.

God, please. Tell me I've lost them. Eluded them. Tell me I'm—

The earth beneath her feet fell away, and she let out a cry as she toppled headlong down a slope and slid to a halt on her belly. Gasping, she rested her cheek against the damp earth, closed her eyes, and gave freedom to her tears. In her mind, she capitulated to whatever fate awaited. She'd reached her limit.

"I can't," she whispered, defying a little voice inside that insisted she keep going. "Please forgive me, but I can't."

As she lay there, her overwrought senses slowly revived—a blessing and a curse. Pain hammered out a relentless rhythm in her shoulder. Dampness seeped through her robe and chilled her skin. The pungent scent of the earth teased her nostrils. A wisp of cool air brushed her cheek and caressed her hair. And from somewhere overhead, a robin chirped out his merry song.

Then all at once, the bird felt silent, his song interrupted by a rustle of movement in the undergrowth. A presence. A soft footfall on the forest floor.

A chill crawled across Breanna's scalp. Her frantic flight had been for naught. They had found her. She offered up a silent prayer, lifted her head... and looked directly into a pair of familiar, amber eyes.

"Theo." She hiccupped on a sob. "Oh, Theo. Thank God."

Chapter Three

Later that same day.
The western border marches of Northern England

Streaks of grey haze threaded through the trees like ghostly fingers, their touch stinging Gabriel's eyes and making his nostrils flare. No benign mist, this, but acrid smoke, bearing the ominous stench of destruction. A decaying stench, too, he surmised—the dwindling secretions of a fire that had wandered from afar. It appeared to be drifting from the southwest, though he could only wonder at its precise origin. Had conflict or ill-fortune been the cause? The former, he suspected.

He'd been forewarned about the inherent dangers of this marcher terrain. The Scottish-English border sliced across Britain's northern lands like an old war wound, festering with violent skirmishes. Gabriel had crossed into English sovereign territory on the cusp of dawn, but with the day already half-gone, he'd yet to see any sign of trouble.

Till now.

Kadar released a throaty rumble, as if agreeing with his master's thoughts.

Keeping his senses alert, Gabriel glanced around. This expanse of greenwood was a pretty, sheltered place—a testament to spring's recent arrival. A bright carpet of bluebells stretched out in all directions, filling the spaces between stout columns of oak and elm, and sweetening the air. Here and there, fronds of bright green bracken, freshly unfurled, reached skyward.

But appearances could be misleading. Terrain such as this also provided sanctuary for outlaws and lent itself to the risk of ambush. So far, the only imminent threat appeared to be from above, where ashen clouds hurtled across the sky, driven by a wind held aloft by the woodland canopy. Gabriel peered up through the branches. Though hidden, the sun was already past its apex. He turned his thoughts, briefly, to where he might find shelter that night.

All such thoughts vanished as the thunder of approaching hoofbeats reached his ears. He straightened in the saddle and surveyed the road ahead. Moments later, a group of horsemen barrelled around a curve in the trail, their horses' hooves sending pellets of mud flying. At the sight of Gabriel, one of the men stood in his stirrups and raised a hand. In unison, the riders pulled their horses to a sliding halt, forming a barrier across the path.

Kadar set his ears back and chomped at the bit, displaying his disapproval. "Easy, my friend," Gabriel murmured, urging the gelding onward. "Let's see what they're about."

The group comprised five men, all armed and mounted on powerful horses. On a mission, seemingly, and not one of a leisurely nature. The man who'd bid them halt stood out as their commander, placing his horse ahead of the others, front and centre. A nobleman of some standing, judging by his attire and the chevron crest emblazoned on his tabard.

Gabriel placed his right hand on his thigh as he drew near, a gesture that curbed a temptation to reach for his sword.

The commander's mouth lifted a smidgen. "A wise decision, Templar," he said, his gaze dropping to Gabriel's weapon. "If that is truly what you are."

"What gives you cause to question it?" Gabriel asked, keeping his expression composed.

"Your blatant lack of prudence," came the reply. "Those white vestments are eyed with suspicion rather than admiration these days."

"Suspicion based on untruths and hearsay." Gabriel lifted his chin. "And I do not wear the mantle to gain admiration."

The man arched a brow. "I will know your name, where you've come from, and where you're going."

Gabriel assessed his inquisitor. Of average height and middling years, the man had a solid, warrior's physique. Lank, dark-brown hair, smudged with silver at the temples, tumbled to his shoulders. His nose, which appeared to have been broken at least once, offset his otherwise proportioned facial features. The sharpness of his gaze implied intelligence, shrewdness, and the glimmer of genuine curiosity.

But no real malice.

"And I will give you the answers you demand," Gabriel replied, "once I know to whom I am speaking."

One of the henchmen—a hefty, square-faced brute—growled an objection. "You will answer my lord without further—"

The nobleman raised a hand once more, silencing the interrupter. "You're speaking to Baron Savaric de Sable of Ghyllhead."

Gabriel nodded his acknowledgement. "And you are addressing Brother Gabriel FitzAlan, a knight of the Temple these past ten years. I am coming from the priory in Carlisle and travelling to Furness Abbey."

"What business had you at the priory?"

"None. I crossed the border yesterday afternoon and merely sought shelter in Carlisle for the night."

"The border, you say?" De Sable's eyes narrowed. "What business had you in Scotland?"

"I was exiled there." The answer tasted bitter. "These past seven months."

"Ah." Comprehension flickered across the man's face. "From France."

Gabriel nodded. "We had advance warning of the arrest and managed to escape."

"We?"

"Myself and two of my Templar brothers."

"And where are they?"

"They remain in Scotland."

"So, what takes you to Furness?"

"I mean to take my vows."

The corner of De Sable's mouth furled as he glanced again at Gabriel's weapon. "You're putting your sword down?"

Gabriel's gut tightened. "I am."

"A pity and a waste." De Sable shifted in the saddle, his expression still sour. "I can always use an extra blade, and those who wield in God's name tend to wield better than most." He heaved a sigh and ran a hand through his hair. "We're seeking a group of renegades who attacked a village on my lands this morning. The smoke you can undoubtedly smell comes from three houses they burned in the attack. They plundered the church, injured the priest, and took…" his jaw clenched, "took my niece captive. 'Tis her we are searching for, though I fear it to be a futile exercise. A woodsman said he saw several riders on this road earlier this morning. Said they appeared to be in a hurry, but didn't notice if they had a captive. Have you heard or seen anything untoward? Anything that struck you as suspicious?"

"I have not," Gabriel answered. "Till now, my day has been uneventful. I suspected the smoke to be from a skirmish. I was told they are common hereabouts."

"And becoming more so of late." De Sable grimaced and rubbed his neck. "I don't suppose, by chance, you've seen any foxes on your travels?"

"Foxes?" Perplexed, Gabriel shook his head. "Nay, I—"

"Never mind." De Sable heaved a sigh and then addressed his men. "Move aside. Let him pass."

Gabriel heard a measure of despair in the man's voice and toyed with an urge to offer assistance in their quest. But this was their fight. Not his. And he silently agreed that their chances of finding the girl were next to impossible. Those responsible had likely gone to ground long since.

"I pray you find your niece unharmed, my lord," he

said, easing Kadar forward.

"May your prayer be heard, Templar." De Sable gathered up his reins and eyed Gabriel up and down. "Should you need somewhere to lay your head this eve, you'll be welcome at Ghyllhead. It overlooks the village of St Bega, on the southwest side of the Kendal road, near Penrith. Barring incident, you should be in that area by day's end." He glanced skyward. "I don't know if we'll be back before nightfall, so if you do decide to partake of my hospitality, ask for Walter at the gate and tell him you spoke with me."

Gabriel inclined his head. "I appreciate the offer, my lord, and will think on it."

"I hope you act on it." De Sable gestured to Gabriel's sword. "I should like the opportunity to dissuade you from surrendering that blade of yours."

With that, he gave a curt nod, spurred his horse into a canter, and tore off down the trail with his men at his back.

Gabriel watched them leave before urging Kadar onward. The encounter had added weight to his thoughts. He'd been right about the smoke having hostile origins, and he wondered at the fate of De Sable's niece. He doubted she'd be harmed. Ransomed, more like. Gabriel could only guess at her age, but assumed her to be of tender years. A maid or even a child.

May God help her.

"Foxes." He pondered De Sable's odd remark, unable to fathom the meaning behind it. The answer might be learned if he chose to accept the man's offer of hospitality, though it held little appeal for him, in truth.

Since Gabriel had left Castle Cathan, most of his nights had been spent within the sanctified walls of a church or priory. He craved the solitude and peace such places offered. Places where he might meditate undisturbed, consider his future, and continue to assure himself of his chosen path. To give himself wholly to the service of God was surely the right choice.

Aye, the right choice.

Not for the first time since he'd set out on his journey, a whisper of doubt rose up from Gabriel's heart. In truth, he still found it near impossible to imagine a world without the Templar order, and uncertainty about his future plagued him. He raised his eyes heavenward, to where an unruly wind still rattled the treetops. "Guide me," he muttered, crossing himself. "Show me."

A gloomy pall descended over the forest as the afternoon waned, which befitted Gabriel's increasingly solemn mood. The fingers of smoke had dissipated, and the bluebells had long since been edged out by swathes of wild leeks. Gabriel breathed in their pungent aroma as he leaned forward to pat Kadar's sleek neck. "We'll stop in a little while, my friend," he said. "You need a res—"

He tugged the horse to a sudden halt, a move prompted by the sight of a creature emerging from the undergrowth onto the road ahead. Normally, he'd have paid the sighting little mind, since such things were not uncommon in field or forest. Indeed, on any other day, the encounter might have drawn nothing more than some mild interest from him. Today it aroused a stronger reaction, one borne from an odd question asked earlier that day by a man seeking to retrieve his captured niece.

'Have you seen any foxes on your travels?'
Not till now.

The fox paused in the middle of the road, sniffing at the air as it stared at Gabriel. It appeared to be appraising him. *Assessing* him. Certainly, it showed no fear. Odd behaviour for a wild creature.

Gabriel sharpened his senses and squinted into the surrounding trees, seeking any sign of movement, but nothing stirred. The only disturbance came from above, where the breeze continued to ruffle the forest canopy.

The fox let out a yip, drawing Gabriel's attention once more. As he watched, the creature turned a tight circle as if chasing its tail, and then scampered back into the woods. Moments later, it reappeared and appraised him once more before repeating its strange, tail-chasing ritual.

The fox's intended message, while barely conceivable, seemed quite clear.

Follow me.

"What devilry is this?" Gabriel murmured, casting another quick glance about. Despite his misgivings, he neither saw nor felt any reason for alarm, and sheer curiosity countermanded caution. Pulling his sword, he dismounted, took Kadar's reins, and followed the fox into the trees.

The creature, bushy tail waving and tongue lolling, ambled off as if certain of his direction, leaving Gabriel and Kadar to pick their way across the forest floor. They had not gone too far when the fox halted and turned to look at Gabriel, who paused as he drew near.

"What?" Frowning, he glanced about. "What are you trying to tell—?"

A faint noise to his left had him spinning on his heel, sword raised in readiness as he searched for the source.

He found it.

Found *her*.

Huddled in a hollow between the gnarled roots of a nearby oak, a young woman stared at Gabriel through wide eyes. Her chest rose and fell in an exhausted rhythm, accompanied by a faint rasp of breath. Several bloody scratches marred the muddied flesh of her face and throat. An assortment of woodland debris adorned her hair, which fell almost to the floor in a chaotic mass of brown curls. Trembling visibly, the woman recoiled, tucking her legs more securely beneath her skirts, wincing as she did so. Her muddied hands, fingers furled, rested atop her knees.

Her wrists, Gabriel realized, were cruelly bound.

"Christ have mercy," he muttered, a suspicion of the girl's identity already settling in his brain. *Can it be*? He dropped Kadar's reins, sheathed his sword, and drew his dagger. As he approached, the girl's chest rose once more, but this time did not fall, and her eyes widened further.

"Don't be afraid," Gabriel said, crouching at her feet. "I mean you no harm."

Frowning, he examined the wealth of welts and scrapes that crisscrossed her face and neck, as well as a patch of dark, crusted blood at the corner of her mouth. Though visually troubling, the wounds appeared to be superficial—evidence of a frenzied flight through the forest. Oddly, what bothered Gabriel more were the dried tracks of tears across her muddied cheeks.

What terror has this girl endured?

She continued to stare at him more in disbelief, it seemed, than fear.

Gabriel held up the knife. "I'm going to remove your bonds. All right?"

She glanced past him to where the fox sat, released the breath she'd been holding, and gave a single nod. Gabriel raised a brow and couldn't help but pose the question. "I take it your friend approves?"

Her reply came without hesitation or flippancy. "He would not have led you to me otherwise."

Lost for a suitable rejoinder, Gabriel moved closer and took the woman's hands in his. They felt like chilled clay.

"Keep very still," he said, and eased his blade beneath the dried strip of leather that bit into the woman's flesh. With a gentle twist and a tug, the blade sliced through the offensive bond, which fell away revealing vicious marks. The girl released a soft hiss.

"Thank you, sir." Her chin trembled as a glimmer of tears arose in her eyes. "I tried to loosen it with my teeth, but the knot was too tight."

"What's your name?" Gabriel rose and sheathed his dagger before turning to untie a rolled blanket from the back of Kadar's saddle.

"Breanna." She drew another audible breath. "Breanna Glendenning."

"Breanna," Gabriel repeated, and turned back in time to see the girl's fleeting expression of pain as she tried to make a fist. He shook the blanket out, settled it about her shoulders, and then crouched before her again. "Give me your hands, my lady," he said, extending his own. Without hesitation, she did as he asked. Gabriel set about manipulating her cold flesh, gently rubbing and kneading to encourage the return of blood.

Though grubby, her hands felt soft to the touch, unblemished by calluses. The fine weave and cut of her clothing further convinced Gabriel of her likely identity, despite the difference in the family name. In any case, he had no doubt he knelt before a gentlewoman, one whose dishevelment did not mask her prettiness. A maid, it seemed, since her slender fingers bore no token of marriage.

That assumption raised a delicate question about injuries he could not see. For now, though, he pushed it to one side. Such enquiries could wait. The girl was visibly exhausted and in obvious distress. For now, she needed more immediate assistance.

"You're a Templar," she said.

"Aye."

She drew a shaky breath. "And I have yet to learn *your* name."

"My name is Gabriel."

"Gabriel." She dropped her gaze momentarily as if tasting the word on her tongue. "You are surely Heaven sent, sir. The answer to a prayer."

Gabriel didn't care to agree or disagree, since neither choice sat well with him. Instead, he nodded toward the fox. "And what is his name, assuming he has one?"

"I call him Theo," Breanna replied, her smile wobbly, "but if you ask the same question of my uncle, I fear he might provide you with several different epithets."

Gabriel continued to rub the girl's hands. Already, her flesh felt warmer. "Would your uncle be Savaric de Sable, by any chance?"

She gasped. "How could you know that?"

Ah. I was right.

"I met him and some of his men on the road earlier today. He was looking for you. He told me about your abduction and asked if I'd seen any sign of you." Gabriel glanced at Theo. "Or him."

"Oh!" Tears welled in the maid's eyes. "Did he say anything else about the attack? Was anyone hurt, or worse?"

Gabriel frowned. "He said three houses had been burned, the church plundered, and the priest injured."

"Father Dunstan was injured?" A couple of stray

tears escaped down her cheek. "Did my uncle say how badly?"

Fighting a temptation to brush the girl's tears away, Gabriel focused his attention on her hands. "Nay, I'm afraid he didn't."

"Oh, I pray he is not seriously hurt. The attack was cowardly, aimed at those who had no defence."

He lifted his gaze as another question arose in his mind. "You had no bodyguard?"

"Nay, I…" A blush came to her cheeks. "I went to the church unaccompanied."

"I see," Gabriel replied, noting her obvious embarrassment. "A furtive venture, I suspect."

"A foolish one." She heaved a sigh. "My uncle will be furious."

"Perhaps. But also relieved that you're safe." He released her hands, wondering how she'd managed to escape her captors. "Better?"

"Much." She clenched and unclenched her fingers. "My thanks, sir."

Gabriel's attention shifted to a filthy, knotted piece of fabric that sat loosely about the girl's slender neck. He realized what it was and bit back a fresh surge of anger. "Let me remove that also," he said, and untied the gag that was spotted with blood and still damp from her saliva.

She grimaced as he cast the offensive cloth aside. "Thank you. I'd forgotten about that."

"'Tis plain you've been brutally treated, my lady," he said, steeling himself to voice an unpleasant question. "Which compels me to ask if you have injuries aside from those I see. Were you otherwise harmed by these men?"

A crease settled between her brows. "I was not violated, sir, if that's what you mean. But I've injured my shoulder. It hurts terribly when I move my arm."

The girl's forthrightness impressed Gabriel. That her innocence remained intact gave him more relief than anticipated. "Which shoulder?" he asked. "And how did it happen?"

"My right shoulder. I hurt it falling from my captor's horse, though I'm not sure precisely *how* it happened, because I was blindfolded, but I believe the animal stumbled and we were thrown to the ground. The man who held me did not survive. I heard..." her teeth chattered, "I heard the snap of his neck when he fell. The other raiders were out of sight, but not far behind us. At least, I heard shouting, so I assume it was them. I didn't wait to find out, which is why I didn't have time to free myself. I ran into the woods, and..." The pitch of her voice heightened and fresh tears arose in her eyes "I just kept running till I could run no further."

"You're safe now, my lady." Gabriel softened his tone. "And I need to examine this injury you speak of, with your permission.

She nodded, and he leaned in to probe the line of her collarbone. Though he took care to be gentle, she flinched at his touch.

"I don't doubt it is painful." His examination continued. "But... I can find no evidence of a fracture. I suspect the bone is bruised rather than broken. For now, try to keep your arm bent at the elbow and hold it close to your body. No sudden movements."

A flicker of admiration arose in her eyes. "You seem to know much about healing, sir."

"Some." He rose. "Are you thirsty? Hungry?"

"Thirsty, yes." She pushed an errant curl from her eyes. "But I have no stomach for food."

Gabriel caught a hint of a floral scent as he turned away, and a memory rose up from the past like a forgotten dream. Time had eroded the finer details, but he recognized the woman in the image as his mother, though she was more shadow than substance. She sat in a chair, talking, her words muffled as if a door lay between them. The soothing tone of her voice, though, was unmistakable.

Despite losing her at a young age, Gabriel possessed other memories of the woman who had birthed him—vague recollections he could bring to mind if he so chose. Till now, however, he'd never associated a perfume with her. Perhaps it had been a dream after all, although that didn't explain how it had been resurrected by a scent.

Hiding his bewilderment, he retrieved his flask and handed it to Breanna, acknowledging her mumbled thanks before digging a small wooden pot from the same saddlebag.

"What is that?" she asked.

"Ointment." He pulled the bung free. "For the scratches on your face."

"Oh." She blinked and touched her tear-stained cheeks. "Are there many of them?"

"Nay, not many, nor do they give me concern, but I'd like to keep it that way. The ointment will protect against the risk of infection." He glanced up at the dimming skies. "Then we should be on our way if we intend to arrive before nightfall."

The flask paused on its way to her mouth. "You're taking me home?"

He cast her a bemused glance. "Where else?"

A sheepish expression settled on her face. "Indeed. But it occurs to me that you'll be delayed from reaching your intended destination."

Gabriel heard the question hidden in her reply but didn't feel like explaining his intentions. "I'm not at the mercy of time, my lady. I can resume my original path on the morrow."

"Yes, of course." The wobbly smile reappeared. "That's... that's good."

She drank, wincing a little as she did so, and then remained quite still as Gabriel dabbed ointment on her scratches and scrapes. Once again, he caught a hint of her scent, though it soon vanished behind the garlicy smell of the ointment.

His vow of celibacy didn't make him blind. Being this close to the girl, touching her, Gabriel could not help but notice detail; the curl in her dark lashes, tiny flecks of gold in her grey eyes, the slight pout of her lips, and the graceful contours of her cheeks and jaw. It was, he allowed himself, a forgivable intimacy, brought about by unfortunate circumstances.

At last, he finished and rose to his feet, relieved to put a little distance between them. "Can you stand, my lady?"

She heaved a sigh. "I think so."

Gabriel bent and cradled her left elbow as she struggled to her feet.

"Oh," she muttered, and reached for him as she swayed. "Dizzy."

"Take your time," he said, taking her hand. "Find your balance."

Gabriel glanced at the fox, who responded by rising to his feet and wagging his tail. It had been a fateful day. One might even wonder if the events of it had been aligned by a greater power. Or perhaps it was nothing more than happenstance. In any case, it seemed Gabriel would be spending the night at Ghyllhead after all.

Chapter Four

Breanna knew of the fate that had befallen the Templars in France. The news, while shocking, had simply been one more disturbing event in a world already full of strife, and Breanna had not dwelt overly long on the sad consequences. She dwelt on them now, steering her thoughts away from the depths of her own despondency.

The persecution of the Templar Knights had now leached into England, though it was rumoured King Edward gave the accusations of heresy far less credence than his French father-in-law. So far, the arrests on this side of the narrow sea had been few, and the interrogations half-hearted, with little retribution. Breanne hoped, for Gabriel's sake, that Edward's lukewarm response to Philip's edict would continue.

A Templar knight was the last person she might have expected to come to her aid—and brought to her by Theo, no less! Never would she have thought the little fox capable of such a feat, especially since the creature, as a rule, placed his trust in no man. So, what was it about *this* man that had engendered the animal's confidence?

Gabriel.

The white mantle declared the knight's allegiance but, other than his name, she knew nothing of him. He had not said where he'd come from. Nor had he disclosed his intended destination, despite her covert attempt to discover it. To ask him such questions outright seemed ungracious, somehow. As for his age, she guessed him to be close to thirty summers, give or take. He seemed possessed of a quiet, even sombre nature. He spoke when necessary, but did not waste words or open himself to trivial conversation. Something of a pity, she thought, since his voice had a deep resonance that both warmed and chilled her. Was it wrong to admit she liked the sound of it? Then again, Breanna also found comfort, rather than awkwardness, in their shared silence.

Gabriel's fine physical condition was unquestionable—she had felt his strength when he'd lifted her into the saddle as if she weighed no more than a child—but he also exuded a fortitude that had naught to do with muscle. Though subtle, it warned against mistaking his calm demeanor for weakness. Breanna guessed it would be foolish to underestimate him.

For now, he walked alongside her, leading the horse. Breanna had initially protested at the arrangement, insisting that he didn't have to walk at all. She could sit behind him, she pointed out, atop the leather saddlebags which straddled the animal's rump.

"It befits me to walk, my lady," he'd insisted, his undertone raising comprehension in Breanna's mind and a subsequent flush of colour to her cheeks. The knight had provided chivalrous aid and would undoubtedly provide his protection. But he was a Templar, and she was a woman. Enough that he had revived her half-dead hands, examined her shoulder, and dabbed some garlic-infused ointment here and there on her face and neck. His concern had been sincere, his touch gentle. Breanna's cheeks warmed anew at the recollection.

She had not pressed her argument. In truth, she had neither the heart nor the strength for it. Besides, she guessed it would be naught but a futile exercise, and perhaps even disrespectful to the man's discipline.

She cast yet another furtive glance at her enigmatic saviour, the waning light giving ghost-like prominence to his pale attire. A tumble of near-black hair brushed his shoulders, framing a face that appeared to have been permanently hued by the sun. He was not bearded, though a faint shadow of stubble outlined his jaw. Breanna tried to recollect the colour of his eyes, but her weary mind refused to surrender such detail. In any case, she couldn't deny the knight's comely appearance.

Given his angelic name, Breanna thought she might be justified in attributing some kind of celestial intervention to his arrival. She had already thanked God a dozen times for sending him to her. For sure, she'd have struggled to make it back to Ghyllhead on her own, bound and exhausted as she was.

With that thought, despondency returned; a torrent of anguish that flooded her heart and mind. A lump, hard as stone, formed in her throat and she turned away. Shivering beneath the Templar's blanket, she feigned interest in the surrounding woodland as tears scorched her eyes. Her shoulder throbbed incessantly and her limbs felt drained of substance. It took all she had to stay upright in the saddle.

Hold on, Breanna. Hold on.

She straightened her aching spine and swallowed. "What is his story?"

Startled and blinking away tears, Breanna turned her gaze back to Gabriel. "Whose?"

"The fox," he replied, his attention on Theo, who still trotted alongside, tongue lolling. "I'm curious to know where you found him."

"Oh." She sniffed and gave her damp eyes a surreptitious swipe. "Um… I actually found him in the village church, hiding behind the altar."

Gabriel gave her an incredulous look. "What was he doing in the church?"

"Seeking sanctuary, I suspect," Breanna replied. "My uncle and some of his men had gone on a chase that morning. The hounds made several kills, including a vixen and her cubs, who were killed on the outskirts of the village. I'm of the belief that Theo managed to escape the dogs and sought safety 'neath the roof of St Bega's."

"So, you raised him?"

She shook her head. "Nay, 'twas Artemis, my uncle's prized hunting bitch, who took the place of Theo's mother. She had recently whelped and readily adopted Theo as one of her pups, much to my uncle's disgust. An enemy in the ranks, he said, and declared Artemis a traitor." Breanna wrinkled her nose and managed a smile. "I prefer to think of it as an atonement."

A return smile flitted across the knight's face and then disappeared as he regarded the fox once more.

"But I have yet to fathom how he came to be with you in the forest today. Did he follow your captors?"

"He must have." The lump in Breanna's throat hardened further as she struggled to keep her tears at bay. "After I escaped, I'm not sure how far I'd run or for how long, but at one point, I stumbled and fell. I confess, I was so tired by that time, I'd given up. But then Theo appeared out of nowhere, as if he'd been with me all along. Seeing him gave me the strength to keep going."

"Remarkable" Gabriel muttered, his expression now thoughtful. "As loyal as any domestic hound."

"Not precisely." Breanna suppressed another shiver and pulled the blanket tighter. "He might have been raised by a domestic dog, but he's only partly tame. Once he'd been weaned, I set about introducing him back to the forest. Whenever I leave Ghyllhead, though, he always shows up at my side. I swear he watches over the place."

"Then why not keep him at Ghyllhead? It would be safer for him to remain there, would it not?"

"Perhaps, but that's not where he belongs." She glanced about. "I believe there's a place for everything under Heaven, and out here is Theo's place. This is his heritage and his legacy."

"Yet, he would likely not be here at all had you not found him."

"And had I not found him, you might not have found me. But I did find him, and here you are!"

And I thank God for you both.

A slight frown crossed the Templar's brow, and his

stride slowed as he appeared to assess her. His eyes, Breanna noticed, were a deep, dark blue. His frown deepened as he halted the horse. "How much farther to Ghyllhead?"

"Um, an hour's ride yet. A little more, perhaps. It lies two miles beyond these woods, to the south-west." Breanna's teeth chattered as she looked up at the sky. "We'll be there before dark, I'm sure."

He muttered something under his breath and tossed the reins over the horse's head. "I'll be riding with you the rest of the way."

Breanna blinked. "Of course," she said. "I'm sure you must be weary."

Something akin to a smile played on his mouth as he unhooked the saddlebags and set them across the horse's withers.

"'Tis not because I'm weary, my lady." He stuck his foot in the empty stirrup and swung onto the horse's back, settling himself behind the saddle. Then, to her great surprise, he wrapped his mantle, and his arms, around her. "'Tis because you are. Lean back. Rest against me."

"Oh, nay, 'tis not necessary, sir." She fidgeted. "I'm not tired. I'm… um… I'm just…"

"Exhausted." He bent his head to hers. "It's all right, Breanna. Lean back."

His breath brushed across Breanna's left ear, sparking a shiver of a different kind. This one ignited a flush of heat that rose up her neck and flooded her cheeks. Thankful Gabriel couldn't see her flustered response, she did as bidden, till that moment unaware of how tense her muscles had been. Stifling a groan of relief, Breanna surrendered to her fatigue and settled against him. He smelled of stale sweat and horse, but she sank willingly into the warmth and refuge of his embrace.

"Thank you, sir," she said, her voice breaking. "I can surely never repay your kindness this day."

Gabriel's chest rose and fell against her as he gathered up the reins and urged his horse onward.

Chapter Five

Surrounded by a snakelike coil of grey curtain wall, the limewashed walls of Ghyllhead Castle loomed out of the evening dusk. It sat atop a rise at the narrow end of a quiet vale. At its feet, an uneven patchwork of grassy meadows and ploughed fields stretched away into the twilight. On its western side, a cluster of thatched dwellings and utility buildings nestled around the grey silhouette of a small church.

And circling it all was an ancient array of bare Cumberland fells, their tops buried in cloud.

From some obscure place in the distance came the mewling wail of an infant. The meadows rang with the throaty bleating of sheep mingled with the softer responses of their lambs. The wind had all but died, though an occasional wisp of air carried odours of freshly turned manure and cooking fires. Ominous hints of burned wattle and thatch also dallied here and there, reminders of the violent events of the day. Despite a faint smell of garlic from the ointment that covered her scratches, Breanna's soft rose scent endured overall, soothing in its delicacy.

That, and being so physically close to the girl, had Gabriel's heart beating a little faster—a sensation he did not welcome. But, by God's good grace, he could justify his actions. Breanna's suffering had not gone unnoticed, and neither had her brave attempts to hide it. If anything, he should have been more mindful and acted sooner. She'd been in need of comfort—more accurately, warmth—and, prompted by echoes of a voice from his past, he had provided it.

To show compassion, Gabriel, is a strength. Never a weakness.

Other than a whisper of thanks, Breanna had said not a word since she settled into his embrace. Gabriel, unsure of whether she slept or not, had respected her silence and made no effort to engage her. Besides, he had little fondness for forced or idle chatter. It was enough that the girl's shivering had ceased and the tension had left her body. She appeared to be warm and at ease, resting against him.

He inhaled her soft fragrance once more and silently admitted relief that their journey's end was in sight. He needed to find a quiet corner—a chapel, preferably. A place to pray and reflect on the day's events. At that moment, the church bell began to toll, and the girl stirred as if from sleep.

"Theo has gone?" she asked, glancing down.

"Before we left the forest," Gabriel replied, "though I confess I didn't see him leave. How do you feel?"

Breanna drew a sigh, sat straighter in the saddle, and brushed her hair back from her face. "Afraid." The direction of her gaze shifted toward the village and the small church at its heart. "Afraid that others might not have fared as well as I. 'Tis reassuring to hear the bell, though, assuming 'tis Father Dunstan who tolls it."

As they turned onto the thoroughfare leading to the castle, a shout went up from the gatehouse, followed by a rattle of chains, moments later, as the portcullis clanked upwards. Before it had even risen halfway, a man ducked beneath it and then paused, his hand resting on his sword hilt. Clad entirely in gray, he blended into the light like a colorless ghost, straggly hair and beard giving him a wild, unkempt appearance.

"My lady!" The man crossed himself as he strode forward, limping slightly.

"Walter MacFayle," Breanna said, answering Gabriel's unspoken question. "My uncle's steward. He can be abrupt at times, but he's not unkindly."

Mumbling unintelligibly, the steward approached and cast an incredulous gaze over them. "My lady," he said again. "Thank the Lord. I can scarce believe my eyes. You are unharmed?"

"My injuries are insignificant, Walter," she replied. "But what of the others? Was Father Dunstan badly hurt? Was anyone injured?"

"We have several with minor wounds, but none dead, thank God. Three cottages razed, though, and the church plundered, damn their heathen souls. Father Dunstan is bruised about the face, but not seriously hurt." The steward's gaze fell to Gabriel. "I would know your name, Templar. 'Twould seem we are indebted to you for the lady's rescue and safe return. I'm curious to know how that came about."

"My name is Gabriel Fitzalan," he replied, tussling with a mildly agitated Kadar, who undoubtedly sensed the promise of some oats, "and Lady Breanna escaped her captors unaided. I have merely escorted her home and would ask that you let us pass without further delay. The lady's injuries are not serious, but need attention nonetheless."

"Of course." The man moved back and fell into step beside them as he addressed Breanna once more. "Your uncle is not here, my lady. He left this morning to search for you and has not yet returned."

"Yes, I know," Breanna replied.

Walter raised his grey brows. "How so?"

"I met Lord de Sable and his men on the road earlier today," Gabriel explained as they passed beneath the portcullis. "'Twas only later that I found Lady Breanna."

"Theo led him to me," Breanna added, "otherwise I would likely not be here now."

"Theo?" Walter's brows remained aloft as he appeared to ponder. "By all the saints. 'Twould seem the flea-bitten miscreant has proved his worth after all. Quite remarkable. Did you learn, by any chance, who might have been responsible for the attack, my lady? I understand the cowards wore helms to hide their faces."

"Aye, they did," she replied, and Gabriel felt her body stiffen. "And no, I never learned who they were."

Walter's mouth thinned. "Did anyone speak? Did you hear an accent? Any hint of their origins?"

She nodded. "The man who took me spoke several times. He sounded English."

"And their direction?"

"Northeast, I think."

"I would have assumed them to be Scottish," Gabriel said, confused by the exchange.

"You would be wrong to assume anything without proof, Brother." Walter grimaced. "There are those living among us who sadly play both sides to their advantage and seek to gain from the suffering of others. Undoubtedly, Lady Breanna's capture was intended to bring about a ransom demand, but it is yet too early to lay blame anywhere. An investigation will ensue, no doubt."

A small crowd had already gathered in the bailey, somber yet clearly happy to see the safe return of their lord's niece. As the portcullis clanked its descent, Gabriel took a moment to study his surroundings. As castles went, Ghyllhead would be described as small, but sturdy.

A stone staircase, rising up one level to an arched entryway, fronted the three-storey-high square keep. A number of wooden outbuildings, of the expected sort, huddled against the inner curtain wall. The damp air held onto an odorous brew of smoke, cooking, and the less pleasant stink of human and animal habitation.

Gabriel reined Kadar to a halt and breathed in another helping of Breanna's sweet perfume before dismounting. "Keep your right arm still," he said, reaching for her. "Try not to burden your shoulder."

"What is wrong with it?" Walter asked, frowning.

"'Tis merely bruised," Breanna replied, wincing as Gabriel lifted her down. "In truth, I confess there is not a part of me that does not ache."

"A warm bath will ease the pain from your limbs." Gabriel looked to the steward. "Can it be arranged?"

"Of course," Walter replied. "And the same for you, Brother, if you require it."

Gabriel shook his head. "My thanks, but nay. I would attend to my horse and then seek out a place to pray. Is there a chapel here?"

"There is." Walter gestured toward the main keep. "'Tis the family chapel, but you're welcome to use it. One of the squires will attend to your horse."

"My thanks again, but I'll see to him myself."

"As you wish." The man pointed his chin at an adjacent building. "Those are the stables."

Gabriel acknowledged with a nod and then, drawn by her silence, shifted his attention back to Breanna, who was gazing at the closed portcullis with a troubled expression. In the fading light, the tracks left by her earlier tears stood out like scars on her cheeks. Gabriel felt a tug on his gut and silently cursed those who had hurt her. And, although she had not voiced it, he knew what question occupied her mind.

"From what I saw, my lady, your uncle is a man well able to take care of himself. Nor did he ride alone."

A sigh escaped her. "Even so, I fear I'll not rest till I know he's safe."

At that moment, a cry echoed across the bailey. Gabriel turned to see a woman, skirts lifted and veil flying, scurrying down the steps of the keep. Folks parted as she then hurried across the bailey.

"Linette," Breanna murmured. "My uncle's wife."

Gabriel wondered if he'd imagined the hint of disdain in her tone.

Huffing, and with a hand pressed against her chest, Linette stumbled to a dramatic halt. "Breanna, my dearest girl, thank God you are returned safe. Such a scare we've had! Are you unhurt? Oh, dear heaven, look at your face. What a mess. I pray those scratches will not leave scars."

"Thank you, my lady. I have been assured they will not," Breanna replied.

"How on earth did you manage to escape your captors?" She gave Gabriel a sideways glance. "And who is this?"

Walter cleared his throat. "With respect, my lady, your niece is in need of rest. May we discuss this at more length indoors?"

"Yes, we may, Walter, and it would appear there is much to discuss." Linette's gaze slid toward Gabriel again. "But first I would know who I have beneath my roof."

Gabriel could not deny that Lord de Sable's wife possessed a striking beauty.

A slight flush of pink dusted the lady's cheeks, enhanced, perhaps, by her flight across the bailey. Her finely shaped mouth, slightly upturned nose, and noble jawline, created a visually pleasing visage that drew the eye. An ivory veil floated down to her elbows, and a thick flaxen braid, draped over one shoulder, fell to her waist. With perfectly arched brows raised, she regarded Gabriel through eyes that had a slight, exotic slant. Their colour, a startling turquoise blue, reminded him of the Mediterranean Sea.

But, unlike the Mediterranean Sea, her eyes lacked warmth.

He inclined his head. "My name is Gabriel Fitzalan, my lady."

"A Templar," she said, her gaze flicking over him in blatant interest.

"These ten years."

Her taut brow slackened. "I am Lady Linette de Sable, Lord de Sable's lady wife. It seems, sir, that we owe you a debt of thanks for bringing my niece safely home." She cast a brief glance at Breanna. "She has caused us much worry this day. My husband was beyond solace when he discovered her gone this morning."

"There is no debt to speak of, my lady," he replied, "but I'll accept the hospitality of your household for the night, if offered."

A smile came and went. "You're welcome to it. Settle your horse and then come inside. As for you, Breanna dear, I think a bath is in order. You stink of garlic."

"Thank you again, sir," Breanna murmured, looking decidedly chastised as she moved past Gabriel and fell into step beside her aunt.

"The girl has been fortunate," Walter said, watching them leave, "though she might not think so when her uncle returns. You said her injuries were not serious. I trust that means she is returned to us intact."

"She assured me of it."

"Thank Christ for that at least. I thought de Sable was going to have an apoplexy when he found out she'd been taken. We didn't even know she'd gone missing till Father Dunstan told us, which gave the whoresons a good head-start."

"She's learned a hard lesson. I doubt she'll wander off unescorted again."

Walter huffed. "I wouldn't place a wager on it, Brother. The lass is near as wild as that mangy fox. Always has been. I look forward to hearing how you found her today." He turned to leave, but paused. "Ten years a Templar, eh? Did you serve in the Levant?"

Gabriel gave a nod. "For six years. And you?"

Walter looked startled. "Me?"

"You deny that you were a Templar?"

His expression softened. "Never, though I tend to keep it to myself. How did you know?"

"I didn't for certain." Gabriel shrugged. "I suppose we learn to recognize our own."

"I was injured at Acre." Walter patted his right leg. "Took an Mamluk arrow to the thigh and was sent back to England. Took me nigh on a year to heal, though not enough to be of any real use to the Order, so I left." He glanced about. "I'm of use here. I've always had a head for business, and I've helped to train de Sable's men using some of what I learned as a Templar. Not so nimble in an actual sword fight anymore, though."

Gabriel gave a sombre smile. "He seems like an honorable man."

"De Sable? Aye, he's well respected in these parts." Walter scratched at his jaw. "He'll try to keep you here, you know. He values a good swordsman."

"Aye, he hinted at it when we met." Gabriel patted Kadar's neck. "If you'll excuse me, Brother, this animal needs attention."

"Of course," Walter replied. "If there's anything you require, just ask. The chapel is to your right when you enter the keep."

Having refused the offers of help from two of Ghyllhead's young squires, Gabriel set about tending Kadar, who already had his nose buried in a bucket of oats. Ghyllhead had a fine stable—well organized and clean, with generous stalls for the animals and a dry hayloft above. A number of the stalls were empty, their occupants gone in pursuit of outlaws. Gabriel wondered how Savaric de Sable and his men had fared. He glanced at one of the several small windows, hung with a pale linen curtain that allowed light to enter but kept midges and flies at bay. Daylight, though plentiful at this time of year, had already begun to wane. His mind then drifted, unbidden, to thoughts of Breanna finding relief in the warm, scented water of a bathtub.

Frowning, he shook the thought away and grabbed a handful of straw to brush Kadar down. The horse, still munching, lifted his head and gave his master a look of contentment. "Don't get too comfortable," Gabriel murmured. "We're leaving at dawn."

The horse returned to his bucket and Gabriel settled into grooming the animal, fully aware of the pair of curious eyes above him, watching through a hole in the hayloft floor.

"Unless you have a very good reason, 'tis ill-mannered to spy on people," he said, as he continued to brush Kadar's dusty coat. "If you have questions to ask of me, then ask them. Otherwise, be off with you."

The resulting rustle of hay implied understanding.

"I mean no harm," said a small voice. "'Tis just that I've never seen a Templar knight before."

Gabriel reached in a saddlebag for Kadar's hoof-pick. "That does not justify spying on one."

Another rustle of hay, then, "Is it true what they say? About the Templars, I mean?"

Supressing a sigh, Gabriel bent to clean one of Kadar's back hooves. "I cannot answer that unless you tell me what has been said."

"That they sleep with their clothes on." There came a sniff. "And they don't like women."

Not quite what Gabriel had expected. He straightened and gazed up at a small face complete with bloodied nose. "What's your name, boy?"

A sleeved arm wiped some of the blood away. "Flip."

"Flip?"

"Aye."

"Did you win, Flip?"

The boy blinked. "Win what?"

"The fight."

"Oh." His cheeks reddened. "Nay."

"Shame." Gabriel gestured with his head. "Get down here."

The boy descended the ladder and approached like a dog expecting to be whipped, lowering his gaze as he came to a halt. Gabriel lifted the boy's chin to be met by a pair of wide brown eyes.

"You'll look at me whenever I speak to you," Gabriel said. "All right?"

The lad nodded.

"And you'll answer me using your voice."

A slight frown flitted across the child's face. "Aye."

Gabriel tutted. "My name is Gabriel, and I am a knight, so you will address me either as sir, or Sir Gabriel."

The lad scratched his head. "Aye, sir."

"That's better." Gabriel cast a critical glance over the boy's scrawny features. The nose-bleed, which had all but stopped, was obviously recent. But the faded remains of a bruise lingered around the left eye, and several smaller bruises, barely visible beneath the grime on the boy's flesh, marked his right wrist.

A dark suspicion, aroused by troubling memories from childhood, soured Gabriel's stomach. "Where are your parents, boy?"

"I have none." Another sniff. "That is, I've never had a father, and my Mama died two summers ago. That's when Lord de Sable brought me here to work."

"What work do you do?"

He shrugged. "Whatever Master Cedric tells me to do."

"Master Cedric?"

"Lord de Sable's squire."

"I see." Gabriel suppressed a sigh. "Is Ghyllhead a good place to live?"

He hesitated. "Um, I suppose."

"Lift up your shirt, Flip."

The boy's eyes widened. "Why? Um, I mean, why, sir?"

"Just do as I ask."

His little chest heaved. "I… I'd rather not."

"I mean you no harm. I just want to see if you have any marks on your skin."

A shadow of fear came to his eyes. He shook his head and peered past Gabriel as if looking for someone. "Please sir, I'd really rather not."

Trust, Gabriel knew, had more value than fear. To force the boy into submission would only do more harm to his fragile young soul.

"As you wish," he said, returning his attention to Kadar's hooves. "And in answer to your questions, a Templar knight might sleep with his clothes on if there's a likelihood he'll be called upon to fight. That way, he'll be ready to go into battle without delay. So, it depends where he is and what he's doing. And they do not *dislike* women. Most Templar knights have mothers and sisters that they love. Some even have wives, though the married brothers are not permitted to wear the white mantle."

The boy fidgeted. "Oh."

"Do you know your age?"

"Six summers, I've been told."

Gabriel continued with Kadar's hooves. "There's a horse comb in that saddlebag over there. Go and fetch it."

"Aye, sir."

"Have you ever cared for a knight's horse?"

"Nay, but I know what to do. I've watched others doing it."

"You mean you've spied on them."

"Um, I suppose. Here's the horse's comb, sir."

"His name is Kadar. Do you think you could tend his mane?"

He let out a soft gasp. "Me?"

"Do you see anyone else here?"

"Nay. I mean, aye, I could tend it for sure." His face brightened as if the sun shone on it. "I just need to get a bucket to stand on."

Gabriel bit back a smile as he straightened. "Go and get one, then. And be quick."

"There's one right here," the boy called, moments later. Smiling, he carried it into the stall and set it upside down beside Kadar. "Is he gentle, sir?"

"As long as you don't try to take his oats away, aye."

As the boy clambered atop the bucket, comb in hand, a shadow fell across the doorway. Gabriel looked over to see the two squires approaching. At the sight of Flip perched on the bucket, their jaws dropped.

"What are you doing there, Flip?" one of the boys said, his hands curling into fists. "'Tis not your place to tend to this knight's horse. There's a pile of dung outside the door that needs carting to the midden. See to it."

Flip, his small chest heaving again, glanced at Gabriel with a silent, but obvious, plea for support. When it did not come, disappointment, like a shadow, crept across his face. He stepped off the bucket and held out the comb to Gabriel, who took it.

"I must beg the lad's pardon, sir," the same boy said. "He has little between his ears and forgets his place. He's not a squire, nor is he even trained as a stable-hand. I'd be honoured to finish up the horse for you."

Gabriel regarded the youth, a gangly lad with near-black hair and the juvenile beginnings of a beard. "What is your name, *sirrah*?"

The lad raised his chin. "Cedric Capell, sir. Squire to Lord de Sable."

Gabriel shifted his gaze to the second boy, who was smaller in stature, but more solidly built, with a tangle of chestnut curls atop his head. "And you?"

"Hubald Aldith, sir, Lord de Sable's page."

"Nay, you're not leaving yet." Gabriel placed a gentle hand on Flip's shoulder as the boy moved past him. "There are things here that require an explanation."

"Indeed," Cedric said, glaring at Flip. "To begin, explain how you deceived this good knight into believing you were qualified to tend his horse. You should be whipped for your lies."

"I—" Flip began.

"Since there was no deceit involved, that is not an explanation I require," Gabriel said, fixing a dark glare on the squire. "I am more concerned about the boy's bloodied nose. Can either of you explain how it happened?"

An expression of surprise flitted across Cedric's face, while Hubald shifted on his feet.

"I'm confused by your silence." Gabriel looped his thumbs into his belt and looked from one boy to the other. "I felt certain you'd have an explanation. Especially you, Master Cedric, since you appear to have blood on your knuckles."

Cedric blinked and gave his right hand a surreptitious glance. "Sir, as I said, the boy is dull-brained and needs to learn discipline. My liege lord put me in charge of him to teach him as I see fit."

"As you see fit." Gabriel scratched his chin. "And is your chosen method having a positive effect on the boy's behaviour?"

Cedric cast a dark glance at Flip. "I believe it will, sir, given time."

Gabriel grunted and turned his attention to the second boy. "And what of you, Hubald? Do you condone Cedric's method of disciplining this young boy?"

The lad, who had assumed a sullen look, gave a hesitant nod. "Aye, sir, I do."

"Interesting." Gabriel's smile lacked any levity. "I look forward to discussing it with your liege-lord when he returns. I'm certain he'll be interested to hear how his young knights-in-training are treating those weaker than themselves."

Was it panic or fear that widened the boys' eyes? A little of both, Gabriel suspected.

"Flip is very disobedient, sir," Hubald said, and huffed as Cedric elbowed him in the ribs. "Well, he is. And he's lazy."

"Clumsy, too," Cedric added. "Always falling and bumping into things, which is likely how he got those bruises."

Gabriel narrowed his eyes. "I didn't mention any bruises."

Cedric shuffled his feet. "He always has bruises."

"Is that so." Gabriel regarded Flip. "Do you have bruises, boy? Tell me the truth."

Nodding, the child lowered his gaze.

Gabriel touched the boy's temple. "Remember what I told you."

Flip looked Gabriel in the eye, and answered. "Aye, I do, sir."

"Where are they? Show me."

Lip trembling, he lifted his shirt.

"God have mercy." Gabriel muttered, crouching to inspect the dark rainbow of colours on the boy's chest and stomach. "Turn around, child." The boy did so, exposing a similar pattern on his back.

"As I said," Cedric piped up. "He's clumsy."

"Are you in pain?" Gabriel asked, in little more than a whisper.

"It hurts when I cough or sneeze." The boy shrugged. "And a bit when I lie down."

Gabriel ground his teeth. "I swear this *clumsiness* they say you have will cease this very day. Do you understand me?"

Flip's eyes widened a little. "Can you do that?"

"I can." Gabriel rose to his feet and sharpened his voice. "Now get back on that bucket, little knave, and finish Kadar's mane. When you're done, tidy everything away. I'm going to the chapel."

"But with respect, sir, the lad should not be permitted to tend the horses," Cedric said, scowling. "He is not a squire."

"That is true." Gabriel picked up his sword and settled it around his hips. "But while I'm here, he can act as my page, since I'm in need of one."

A barely suppressed squeak from within Kadar's stall had Gabriel biting back a smile.

"'Tis not my place to question you, sir," Cedric said, his expression sour, "but I feel obliged to point out that the boy is not yours to ennoble. He belongs to Lord de Sable."

"Nay, 'tis not your place to question me, *sirrah*." Gabriel gave the squire a scathing look as he stepped past him. "My actions here will be discussed with your liege-lord upon his return, though I doubt very much he'll object given what has taken place today." He paused. "One more thing. Your mistreatment of the boy will cease from this moment on. And know that I shall continue to oversee his well-being, even from afar. If I hear so much as a whisper that you've resumed your cowardly ways, or if any harm comes to him by your hands, I'll make certain neither of you ever attain the honour of knighthood. Is that clear?"

Chapter Six

The hiss of seared flesh filled the air, followed by a gargled cry of pain and a stench one could taste. Savaric de Sable spat out the piece of wood that had been clenched between his teeth and glared at Gabriel through eyes glazed by copious amounts of wine.

"Sweet Christ, Templar, but you are misnamed as an angel, for you lack any measure of mercy."

Gabriel set the hot iron back in the brazier and scooped up a spoonful of honey from the pot nearby. "Perhaps you would have preferred to bleed to death," he said, spreading a layer of the golden liquid over the sealed flesh, which drew another curse from Savaric. "And I suggest you pray for Christ's blessing rather than taking his name in vain."

"I'll shall continue to blaspheme and leave the praying to you." Savaric, stretched out atop a trestle-table in the solar, tried to sit up. "Are you done with your torture?"

"Nay." Gabriel pushed the man back down. "I still have to wrap the wound."

Savaric growled like a bear. "God curse your bones."

Gabriel ignored the man's surliness, recognizing it as the turbulent offspring of pain and intoxication.

The lord of Ghyllhead had returned around the midnight hour; weary, angry, and bleeding. Gabriel, at prayer in the chapel, had heard the clamour of the men's arrival. Before he'd had time to finish his supplications, the chapel door burst open and Walter had marched in, wearing an expression that pulled Gabriel to his feet.

"You are needed, Brother," Walter had said. "Now."

Gabriel learned that De Sable and his men had tracked down a group of renegades, though it was doubtful they were the ones responsible for Breanna's abduction. An unruly skirmish had ensued before the group had scurried off like rats into the night, a couple of them wounded. Savaric's men had all evaded injury, but Savaric sustained a slash to his sword-arm that had sunk the blade to the bone.

Gabriel knew the cut, while not fatal in itself, could turn deadly if allowed to fester. "You've lost a fair measure of blood," he said, as he fastened off the bandage. "Rest, therefore, is in order. Two or three days at least. And these wrappings must be replaced with clean ones every day and the honey reapplied." He addressed Walter, who had stood by and watched the proceedings. "Do you not have a healer at Ghyllhead?"

"Aye, you." Grimacing, Savaric sat up and swung his legs off the side of the table. "Merciless though you are."

Walter gave his lord a sympathetic glance and responded to Gabriel's question. "There's a woman in the village—Winifred— who has knowledge."

Gabriel nodded. "Then I suggest you summon her in the morning."

"And I suggest you remain at Ghyllhead." Savaric scowled as he rolled his right shoulder. "You have skills in medicine *and* swordsmanship. I beg use of both services till I heal."

"I regret I must refuse, my lord. My destination lies elsewhere."

"The abbey will still be there a few weeks from now." Savaric clenched and unclenched his right hand. "You'll be well compensated."

Gabriel slung the saddlebag over his shoulder. "I do not need your money."

"Then give it to the abbey when you finally get there." Savaric slid from the table and straightened with obvious caution, swaying slightly as he met Gabriel's gaze. "I already owe you a great debt, Templar. I thought Breanna lost and at the mercy of those whoresons. When I found out you'd brought her home, that she was safe beneath this roof, I…" His face contorted as if in pain. "Damn her foolish hide! She might wish you'd left her in the forest by the time I'm done with her tomorrow."

"You owe me nothing, my lord," Gabriel said. "And, in the lady's defence, her regret is not for herself, but solely for you and those involved the attack. Her contrition is sincere."

"And still you protect her." Savaric gave a grim smile. "'Tis brazen of me to ask more of you after all you've done, but I ask it anyway. A few weeks only. You'll take no harm from it, and Ghyllhead will surely gain from your presence and your instruction."

"I told you so," Walter muttered, folding his arms and smirking at Gabriel.

Savaric glanced from one man to the other. "Told

you what?"

"Nothing of import," Gabriel replied, eyeing Savaric's grey pallor with concern. "You really need to rest, my lord, and without further delay."

"Gabriel is right, my lord," Walter said, moving to Savaric's side. "I've seen corpses with more colour. Let me escort you to your chamber. Your lady wife must be frantic with worry by now."

Savaric grunted. "Will you at least consider my request, Templar?"

"That I will do, aye," Gabriel replied, begging silent forgiveness for his deception. There was naught to consider, after all, since the decision had already been made.

He'd be leaving for Furness Abbey in the morning.

Gabriel left his pallet before dawn and headed for the stables, intending to check on Kadar. The cool, night air offered relief after the stagnant atmosphere of the Great Hall. He filled his lungs with it and glanced skywards, where a bejewelled tapestry of stars stretched from horizon to horizon.

The bailey stood empty, not unusual given the early hour. A couple of watchfires burned atop the gatehouse, and those on guard appeared as black silhouettes as they kept vigil on the battlements.

Gabriel paused and looked to the southwest where the great abbey lay. He had never seen it, but he created a vision of it in his mind's eye, hoping to feel the lure of the place. A mild tingle of anticipation trickled down his spine.

Then another vision arose unbidden, this one quite real, and his heart took a sudden leap. It prompted him to look back at Ghyllhead's keep. He'd seen no sign of Breanna since her aunt had whisked her away, and he wondered, for the umpteenth time, how she fared.

She had yet to face her uncle, whose urgent need for aid had delayed any such encounter. Given the man's mood earlier that night, Gabriel feared it might not bode well for the girl. Then again, perhaps Savaric's blood—what remained of it—might have cooled a little by morning.

Before leaving Ghyllhead, Gabriel also had a few things to discuss with Savaric de Sable. The ill-treatment of young Flip, for one thing. The sight of the child's bruised body had disturbed dormant memories, sights and sounds that haunted Gabriel like ghosts. Shaking off unwelcome shadows of the past, he continued on to the stables.

Kadar appeared fed and rested. Ears pricked, he blew a greeting to Gabriel, who heaved a sigh as he stroked the animal's nose. Giving up his horse would not be easy, though he had little choice, since he doubted there'd be a place for him at the abbey. The animal was not suitable for a plough or a wagon. Indeed, such work would be demeaning to him. Kadar was a knight's horse, highly trained. Gabriel would ensure he went to a good master.

"I'm going to miss you, old friend," he murmured, and swallowed against the tightness in his throat.

"Why?" a little voice enquired. "Where are you going?"

Gabriel glanced up to see the pale blur of Flip's face peering through the gap. "You should be asleep," he replied sternly. "And I believe I told you, 'tis ill-mannered to spy on people."

"I'm not spying, sir." A sniff ensued. "I'm guarding your horse."

Solemn by nature, Gabriel did not laugh easily, but he laughed now. "In that case, little knave, I suppose you're excused."

"But how come you'll miss him? Where are you going?"

"To Furness Abbey to take my vows, so I'll have no need of him anymore."

A short period of silence ensued. Then, "When are you leaving?"

The sadness in the boy's voice touched Gabriel's conscience. "Come down here, Flip, where I can see you."

The child appeared moments later, dragging his feet, eyes wide in the gloom. "When?" he asked again.

"In a short while."

"You mean today?" he squeaked, his eyes widening even more.

"Aye."

"Oh." He dropped his gaze and wiped his sleeve across his nose.

Gabriel crouched to better look the boy in the face. "I thought you knew I was only here for the one night," he said, "but I still intend to speak to Lord de Sable about you before I leave. I'll make sure those boys don't bother you anymore."

Flip lifted his chin and met Gabriel's gaze. "Thank you, sir." His lip quivered. "May I return to my bed now?"

"Of course." Gabriel rose to his feet trying, and failing, to recall a time when he'd felt such guilt. "Sleep well. I'll speak to you again in the morning."

Chapter Seven

"She should be whipped." Linette folded her arms as she paced back and forth at the foot of Savaric's bed. "If not for her foolish wanderings, you would not be laying here, wounded and feverish."

"I'm hardly at death's door, Linette. I can still get out of bed to piss." Savaric, propped up against his pillows, frowned as his gaze wandered over Breanna's face and neck. She fidgeted beneath his scrutiny, recalling Gabriel's similar inspection and subsequent treatment of her scratches. Savaric's gaze then dropped to her wrists, where the marks from her bindings could still be seen. "May the bastard rot in Hell," he muttered. "Do they hurt, lass?"

"Nay," she replied, the tremble in his voice bringing tears to her eyes.

"Well, at least they won't leave scars," Linette said, glaring at Breanna and then throwing a pointed glance at Savaric's injury.

"Thank God," Savaric mumbled, causing his wife to huff.

Breanna managed a half-hearted smile. She'd have felt better if her uncle had raged and shouted, demanding apologies and threatening all kinds of repercussions. His blatant concern, his relief at having her home and safe, only added to her burden of guilt.

Because of her thoughtless self-indulgence, the lord of Ghyllhead, the man who had raised her as his own, could no longer swing a sword, or train with his men, or fight off an enemy should the need arise. And during the night, he'd developed a fever.

She silently cursed her foolishness. Her *stupidity*.

"My lady aunt is right to be angry," Breanna said. "I disobeyed you knowingly, my lord, and even commended myself for it. I cannot tell you how much I regret what I did."

Savaric grunted. "The raid would have happened whether you'd been there or not. I'd even venture to say your abduction may have, in fact, lessened the amount of damage done to the village. They left very quickly, and I suspect they did so because they had you."

"'Tis not the damage to the village which concerns me." Linette fiddled with one of her pearl-drop earrings. "'Tis the harm done to you, Husband. You might have been killed."

Savaric gave his wife a withering glance. "But I wasn't. Nor was anyone else, miraculously. And the damage to the village should be as much a concern to you, Wife, as it is to me."

Breanna's mind wandered back to the previous morning. "We've already got more than we came for," she murmured, reflecting on her Uncle's theory.

"What do you mean?" Savaric asked.

"'Tis what he said to one of the other raiders." Her gut clenched at the recollection. "The man who took me."

A knock sounded at the door, making her jump. The subsequent sight of Gabriel on the threshold further caused Breanna's heart to flip. He'd been present in her dreams during the night—a source of light in the shadows. But for some reason, she thought he'd left Ghyllhead before sunrise, and had told herself she'd forever regret not seeing him before he'd departed.

That he was still here boosted her flagging spirit to the point of thankful tears. His eyes widened slightly when he saw her, as if he hadn't expected to see her, either.

"Good day, my lord." His gaze flicked to Linette and then lingered a prolonged moment on Breanna. "Ladies."

He looked weary, she thought, as if he'd had a similar night to her own.

"So," Savaric said, "you haven't abandoned us."

"Not yet. There are things I wish to discuss with you before I leave." A cloth bag grasped in his hand, Gabriel approached the bed. "And I've been told you have a fever. Is that true?"

"It is," Linette said. "I fear the wound is already infected."

Savaric snorted. "'Tis warm in here and I'm sweating. Otherwise, I feel fine. I'd be up and about if I had my way."

"Which would not be wise." Gabriel set the bag atop the bedside table. "With your permission, my lord, I should check the wound for infection."

Savaric shrugged. "By all means."

"Well, if you'll excuse me, I'll take my leave of you." Linette lifted her skirts and moved toward the door. "I wish to discuss a few things with Walter. Is there anything you need, Husband?"

"Nay."

"Then I shall return in a while."

Savaric chuckled as his wife scurried from the room. "'Tis the unwrapping of the wound that has chased her away. She's had a delicate stomach these past few days."

"Do such sights trouble you, my lady?" Gabriel asked, who had already begun to removed the bandages.

"It troubles me to see my uncle in pain," Breanna said, moving closer to him, wondering if he could hear the clatter of her heart. "But I'll not faint at the sight of his injury, if that's what you mean. I'll be happy to assist you with the tending of it, if you have need of me."

"I might," he said, and peeled off the final layer of linen, causing Savaric to suck in a breath.

Despite her declaration, Breanna let out a gasp at the sight of her uncle's wound, its seared surface vicious and raw. She looked up at Gabriel, who was frowning. "It's a horrible colour. Is it infected?"

"There's some weeping, which is to be expected, but there's no discernable stench." He pulled a pot and some clean linen strips from his back. "'Tis early days yet, however. Perhaps you can occupy yourself with your uncle's care after I leave."

Breanna's heart dropped to her shoes. "When are you leaving?"

"You may well ask, child," Savaric said, before Gabriel had a chance to respond. "I believe you owe this man an apology for the distress and inconvenience you have caused."

"I am neither distressed nor inconvenienced, my lord," Gabriel said, frowning. "And I do not require an apology."

"Nevertheless, you'll have one." Savaric grimaced as he shifted his weight. "Breanna?"

She could not argue her uncle's demand, since Gabriel would not be here if not for her. Yet, if truth be told, his presence at Ghyllhead was not something she regretted in the least, despite the circumstances.

"I..." As she met his gaze, a flutter beneath her ribs, like a trapped bird, stole her breath. The celestial blue of his eyes reminded her of the night sky right before dawn—forever her favourite time of day. They seemed to darken as he looked at her, too, as if responding to some hidden emotion. He blinked, bringing her back to full awareness and prompting her to speak, her cheeks warming as she did so. "I truly regret any trouble I have caused you, sir, and beg your forgiveness."

"There is naught to forgive." He gave a wry smile. "And, in truth, it was Theo who interrupted my journey. Not you."

Savaric huffed. "Damned fox."

"But for him, I would not have found your niece, my lord."

"And but for him, I would not have found my way through the woods," Breanna added. "He's been a blessing, Uncle."

Savaric scratched at his chin. "Aye, he's proved his worth, I'll grant you that."

"How's your shoulder?" Gabriel asked, unrolling a clean strip of linen.

"Still sore," Breanna replied. "But less so than yesterday."

"What's wrong with your shoulder?" Savaric asked. "And how come I've not heard of this till now?"

"I injured it when I fell from the horse," Breanna explained. "'Tis bruised only, not broken. An insignificant injury when compared to yours."

"God's teeth. You're lucky you didn't break your neck as well." A tic came to Savaric's right eye. "I'll hear everything that happened to you, child. I would know every detail about your abductor. Everything you can think of. What he wore, how he spoke, what he said. I don't think the men we encountered were the ones we sought. They were just forest rats, feasting on a stolen pig."

Breanna suppressed a shudder. "The man who abducted me is beyond capture, Uncle."

"Aye, but those who rode with him are not. I need to send a report to Lord de Clifford. He's eager to stamp out these cursed raids, and has asked for— shite!" Savaric hissed through his teeth and glared at Gabriel. "God did not bless you with a gentle touch, Templar!"

Gabriel said nothing, but continued to clean the wound. Breanna, who had been on the receiving end of Gabriel's gentle touch, silently disagreed with her uncle's declaration.

"As I was saying," Savaric went on, "De Clifford

requires written reports be submitted. I'll have Walter speak with the villagers, though I'm not sure how much detail, if any, they can supply."

"I'll write my own witness report for Lord de Clifford, Uncle, if you wish," she said, tapping her temple. "I hold all the information, so it makes more sense for me to do it."

Gabriel paused in his ministrations and regarded her. "*You'll* write the report?"

She blinked. "Should I not, in your opinion?"

"Nay. I mean, aye. 'Tis just… unexpected."

"Here we go," Savaric mumbled.

"Why? Because I'm a woman?" She cocked her head at him. "I learned to read and write at a young age, sir, and take great pleasure in it. Are you literate?"

"I am, my lady, and I meant no offence. I also—"

"If you've both quite finished," Savaric said, scowling, "this wound will have healed itself by the time you finish wrapping it."

Gabriel gave Breanna a smile that set her heart racing anew, and resumed his ministrations. "Have you been watching, my lady?" he asked, as he tied off the wrappings.

"I have, sir."

"You'll be able to manage?"

She suppressed a sigh. "I think so."

"Rethink your decision, Templar, and stay a while," Savaric said. "I fail to understand your hurry to get to Furness. God is here too, if you need Him. What is it you wished to discuss with me, by the way?"

"A matter concerning a young boy who works for you."

"Which boy is that?"

"Flip."

"Ah. The orphan. What has he done?"

"Nothing wrong," Gabriel replied. "I'm merely concerned about his wellbeing. I regret I must also report on the behaviour of your squire."

"Cedric? What's he done?" Savaric lifted his wounded arm as if to test it, wincing as he opened and closed his fist. "He's an arrogant little shite. Takes after his sire. But these alliances are necessary, unfortunately."

Breanna listened as Gabriel recounted his story, tears filling her eyes as he described the bruises on the boy's small body. Savaric said nothing the entire time, although Breanna noticed the tightening of his jaw as Gabriel continued.

"I told the boy I would speak with you, and swore that he would not be ill-treated again," Gabriel said, in conclusion. "Can you assure me of that?"

Savaric sighed and regarded Gabriel as if assessing him. "Stay," he said at last. "Three weeks. That is all I ask. Three weeks in which my arm will be given a chance to heal while you take over the training of my men and teach those young reprobates a lesson in discipline and chivalry. I'll give you full rein, Templar. You may do as you see fit, no questions asked. I'll also give you a donation for the abbey. A generous one."

Breanna slid a hand behind her back and crossed

her fingers.

Gabriel heaved a sigh. "Lord de Sable, I regret—"

"I need you." Savaric grimaced as if the admission hurt. "I cannot lift a sword. We've just been attacked. Two houses burned and our priest injured. I really—"

Breanna gasped. "May God forgive me, I forgot all about Father Dunstan. I must go and see him right away."

Savaric shook his head and lifted his eyes to the ceiling. "And I also have a wayward niece, who has apparently not learned her lesson!"

"I had no intention of going alone, Uncle. I'll have Alfred escort me." Keeping her fingers crossed behind her back, she looked at Gabriel. "Or perhaps Sir Gabriel might, if he decides to stay."

Brow furrowed, Gabriel regarded her for a moment. Then his gaze slid back to Savaric. "A fortnight at most," he said, "and not a day longer."

Chapter Eight

"Someone in the village heard him crying and went to investigate." Breanna, clutching a basket, ambled alongside Gabriel as they headed down the lane toward the church. "They found him beside the body of his mother, the poor little soul. His real name is actually Philip, but when he was first brought to the castle, he pronounced it 'Flip', and it has since stuck with him."

"I wondered how he came by it," Gabriel replied, and held out a hand. "Let me take that, my lady. How did his mother die?"

"An ague." She passed the basket to him. "Thank you. We lost several villagers to it that winter, which was a hard one." She shook her head. "I had no idea the boy was being ill treated. Nor did my uncle, I'm sure."

"The child was afraid to tell anyone." Gabriel staved off a familiar sense of anger. "He was told he deserved the beatings."

He felt Breanna's gaze upon him, but resisted meeting it. Doing so had already got him into trouble that day. He regretted— or perhaps, resented— his decision to stay at Ghyllhead. It had been made in a moment of weakness; a capitulation to a plea from a pair of pretty grey eyes that regarded him with undisguised admiration.

He should have reined in his ego.

"I'm glad you came to his defence," she said, "and I'm very glad you'll be staying with us for a while."

She gasped and halted in the road. "Ah, there you are! I was beginning to wonder."

Gabriel watched in renewed amazement as Theo scampered out of the undergrowth and ran to Breanna. The noise the fox made—a series of chirps and squeaks—sounded almost like laughter. For sure, they were sounds of joy. Tail waving, he turned several tight circles and then rolled onto his back, exposing his belly. The animal's obvious delight at seeing his mistress touched Gabriel's heart.

Breanna crouched to pet him. "Theo! My sweet friend. I'm happy to see you too." Smiling she looked up at Gabriel. "See? I swear he keeps watch over me."

"I believe he proved that yesterday," Gabriel replied.

Tongue lolling, Theo righted himself, shook out his red coat, and approached Gabriel, who bent and scratched the fox's head. "Greetings, Theo," he muttered, receiving a wag of the fox's tail in response. "You're a good little soldier."

He straightened, his smile fading as he saw Breanna's shocked expression. "What's wrong?"

"Um…nothing, really." She blinked and shook her head. "I'm surprised, is all. Theo has never let any man touch him before. Not even Father Dunstan."

Gabriel blinked and regarded the fox once more. "Then I suppose I'm honoured."

"Well, you obviously possess some quality that other men do not," she said, and gestured toward the church. "Have you heard of Saint Bega before? She is well known in these parts. I'm not sure about elsewhere in the land."

"Nay, her name is not familiar to me." Gabriel found himself wanting to smile at Breanna's forthright manner. Her lack of coyness probably deserved his disapproval, but instead, it amused him. He found it refreshing rather than objectionable.

She paused in front of the church and looked toward the village.

"'Tis a shame," she murmured. "I fail to see what is gained from such action."

Gabriel followed her gaze to where the charred remains of a cottage could be seen, roof trusses, like blackened fingers, pointing to the sky.

"It creates fear," he replied, recalling the tendrils of smoke he had seen and smelled the day before, not knowing where they'd come from. And now, here he was, looking at the source, or what remained of it. He allowed himself a rare moment of fancy, wondering if this might all be part of some celestial plan.

"Yes." Breanna's sad expression no doubt reflected what lay in her mind. "That it does. 'Tis a cowardly way to fight."

The scratches on her face stood out against the milk-white of her skin, and dark shadows sat beneath her eyes. She looked weary, Gabriel thought. Exhausted.

"I think, my lady, after we've visited the priest, you should retire to your bed for the remainder of the day."

She wrinkled her nose at him. "Do I look that bad?"

His mouth twitched. "You look tired, which is to be

expected."

"As do you, sir. But there's something else I want to show you when we return to Ghyllhead."

"It can wait till tomorrow."

"Aye, it can, but I can't." She shrugged. "Come and meet Father Dunstan. Theo, wait here."

Gabriel gripped the hilt of his sword and silently cursed those who had dared to inflict such injuries upon a defenceless priest. Father Dunstan looked as though he'd collided with a stone wall. A dark rainbow of colour circled his right eye, which was nearly swollen shut. His other eye had a vivid crescent of purple beneath it. And his jaw had a blue and crimson welt that stretched from the side of his mouth to his right ear.

Gabriel watched as the priest brought Breanna's hand to his lips.

"Oh, my dear child," he said, his voice rasping, "I don't believe I have ever prayed as hard in my life, but those prayers have been answered, thank Christ." He examined the welts on her wrist and touched a finger to a scratch on her face. "Did they harm you, other than what I see?"

Breanna shook her head. "Nay, Father," she replied, with a telltale sniff. "And never mind about me. Look what they've done to you! May they rot in Hell, the cowardly bast—"

The priest tutted and placed a finger against her

lips. "Remember where you are, child. I'm sure I look worse than I feel, though I confess to having had better days. And you've brought a visitor with you, it seems."

"I have." She brushed a tear from her cheek and turned to Gabriel. "Sir Gabriel, this is Father Dunstan, the priest of Saint Bega's. Father Dunstan, this is Sir Gabriel Fitzalan, the knight who found me and brought me home."

"Your chivalry is to be commended, Brother Gabriel." Father Dunstan took Gabriel's hand and squeezed it. "Welcome to Ghyllhead, though I regret the circumstances that brought you here. May God bless you for bringing our lady home."

"'Twas my honour, Father." Gabriel handed the basket to him and studied the bruises. "The skin is unbroken?"

"Aye. I think he loosened a tooth, though." The priest waggled his jaw, wincing as he regarded the basket. "And what is this?"

"Salted herring, cheese, and a bottle of mead," Breanna said.

"Bless you, child, though I suspect I'll only be able to cope with the mead for a day or two."

"What did they take?" Breanna asked, glancing about.

"It was only one man, and he took the paten and the chalice," Father Dunstan replied. "It all happened so quickly. I tried to stop him, but he felled me with a couple of punches. I'm not as spry as I used to be."

"You were brave to resist," Gabriel said.

"In hindsight, I was probably foolish." The priest gestured to Breanna. "And I was more concerned about this one. By the time I realized what was happening, it was too late. She'd already been taken. And I hear we owe a certain little creature our thanks as well."

"Theo." Breanna nodded. "I owe him much. He's outside."

"Bring him in if you wish," Father Dunstan replied. "I'll never refuse him entry after this."

"Thank you, Father, but he's likely sunning himself on the step, and quite happy. I wanted to see you, but I also wanted to show off our little church to Sir Gabriel. He has not heard of St Bega."

"Then we must remedy that," Father Dunstan said, with a measure of enthusiasm that did not quite ring true.

"Another day, Father," Gabriel replied, understanding. "You need to rest, as does Lady Breanna. I'll be here a fortnight, so we have plenty of time. Let me know if that tooth troubles you. In the meantime, a cup of mead might be in order."

He waggled his jaw again. "My thanks. I will. And I agree, my lady. You should rest. You look exhausted."

Breanna gave Gabriel a wry glance. "So I've been told." She took the priest's hand and kissed it again. "I'll be by in a day or two, Father."

"Ghyllhead is not the first edifice to occupy this

site," Breanna explained. "It sits atop a much older foundation, a good deal of which remains intact." A halo of candlelight, from the flickering taper grasped in Breanna's hand, travelled with them as they moved along a passageway in the lower level of the keep. "I was in my fifth summer the first time I saw this place. 'Tis the reason I learned to read and write. 'Tis reason I *wanted* to learn."

"I confess you have me intrigued, my lady," Gabriel said, as they came to a stout oak door set flush into the wall.

"I'm sure you'll be impressed, sir." Breanna granted him a smile and then pulled a key from a pouch attached to her belt. She unlocked the door, which swung partly open on its own. To Gabriel's surprise, light could be seen within.

"I expected darkness," he said, as Breanna opened the door wide.

"There's a window." She blew out the candle, stood to the side, and inclined her head. "After you, sir knight."

Gabriel smiled at Breanna's feigned drama. He smiled easily when around her, he'd noticed. Unusual for him. He'd never really grasped the concept of humour, a failing that Ewan, with no ill intent, had blatantly exploited. Which reminded him—he needed to write a letter.

He halted two steps over the threshold, his brain barely able to comprehend what his eyes beheld. He had seen similar sights in the Holy Land, where Rome had maintained a merciless foothold for several centuries. Roman ruins, too, were scattered around the Britannic isles, many of them ravaged by time or reclaimed by nature. But to find a remarkably preserved remnant of the old empire in the bowels of a Norman keep was beyond unexpected.

Speechless, Gabriel moved further into the chamber. The ancient frescoes, once bright with colour, had faded to ghostly outlines on the plaster walls, but their shapes were still discernable. Men and women. Children. Dogs. Oxen. And even a chariot. He looked down at the mosaic floor, the colours still so bright that one might think it had been laid mere weeks earlier.

Only the contents of the chamber identified the current era; an oak cupboard against one wall, a wooden bench against another, a cross hanging above the arched window, and below that, three scribing desks.

"It's a scriptorium now." Breanna moved to stand beside him, her subtle scent sweetening the musty odour of the room. "But Father Dunstan says it was probably a Roman temple at one time."

"'Tis remarkable."

Unsettled by Breanna's nearness, Gabriel moved to where a crucifix hung on the wall. Crossing himself, he gazed at it for a few moments. His liturgies, of late, had been sadly neglected, and his discipline had been lax. He silently pledged to spend more time in the chapel from that moment on, and less time in the solitary company of a young woman.

"You're welcome to make use of it, of course."

Breanna's voice broke into his musing. "If you need parchment, there's some in the cupboard. Ink and quills as well."

"My thanks." He turned back to her. "Who taught you to write, Breanna?"

The smile on her face faded. "My mother."

"Ah. Forgive me. I didn't mean to pry."

"Nay, it's all right. She sickened and died when I was in my seventh summer, so my memories of her are somewhat vague. I remember her voice though, and for some reason, her hands. She had beautiful hands." Frowning, Breanna regarded her own, as if searching for similarities. "Her name was Anna. My father's name was Robert. He was a Scot and died before I was born."

"Which explains your family name."

"Glendenning, yes." Breanna grimaced. "My English grandfather was strongly against the marriage and arranged for Mama to go St. Bees priory, but she defied him and ran away to wed my father. My grandfather was furious. He disowned her and swore she'd never be allowed to set foot on his land again. My parents had only been married three months when my father was killed in a skirmish with the English. His family wanted nothing to do with Mama, so she came back to Ghyllhead and begged my grandfather for mercy."

"And I assume he gave it, since you're here."

"He did, but he barely spoke to her again and refused to acknowledge me as his granddaughter. He died when I was but a year old. That's when Uncle

Savaric assumed lordship. He's been like a father to me." Her eyes widened. "And I can't believe I just told you all that. You're probably not the least bit interested."

Gabriel suppressed yet another smile. "Quite the contrary. We share similar histories, since my mother also died when I was young, and she is also is the one who taught me to write."

Breanna gasped. "What was her name? Not Anna, surely."

"Nay." Images arose in his mind. "Her name was Janette. She was French."

"And your father?"

"He died shortly before I gained my spurs." A cold hand tightened around his stomach. "His name was Ralf. He was a cruel man. I had no love for him."

"Ah." Her face fell. "I'm sorry."

"Don't be." Frowning, he approached her. "I want you to do something for me, Breanna."

Trust shone from her eyes, innocent and valuable. "Of course, sir. Anything."

"I want you to get some rest," he said. "No more excuses. You've been through much, yet all of your attention, thus far, has been given to others, which is admirable, but not without risk. The aftermath of your ordeal will take you unawares if you're not careful."

She appeared chastised. "All right."

Of their own volition, or so it seemed, his fingertips traced a line down her cheek. He wondered if she knew how easily she undermined his resolve. It had been a mistake, agreeing to stay at Ghyllhead. *May*

God help me.
　　"Swear it."
　　Her chest rose and fell. "I swear."

Chapter Nine

Breanna kept her word. She rested for the remainder of that particular day and the entirety of the next. Or at least, she tried to. Sleep had been either elusive or unsettled, her dreams dark and chaotic. If anything, on this third day, she felt even wearier than before.

Needing a diversion, she'd gone to St. Bega's that morning beneath cloudless skies, taking some gooseberry preserve and bread for Father Dunstan, whose bruises had changed from black and blue to purple and yellow. He'd been in good spirits, though, and Breanna had spent the remainder of the morning with him and Theo, who had appeared out of nowhere, as usual.

Alfred had escorted her there and back, much to her secret disappointment. Not that she disliked the man. Alfred had been loyal to her uncle for as long as she could remember and had always treated her kindly.

She'd simply have preferred different company.

But Gabriel had been busy tending her uncle's wound, which had, so far, thankfully, escaped infection. "Be sure to take an escort," her uncle had said, when she'd announced her plans… and she had given Gabriel a hopeful glance.

But he had not offered.

Breanna knew it was madness, of course, this attraction she felt for him. Sinful, even. He was a Templar, a man who'd taken holy vows, and who would soon be on his way to Furness.

But she dared to imagine he felt something for her as well. She'd seen that same darkening of his eyes when they'd been together in the scriptorium. And his touch, as soft as a whisper, had sent a tingle down her spine.

Watching him now, however, one would not believe him capable of such gentleness. The monk, the healer, the scribe had gone. In his place, a warrior trained to kill. A knight of the Temple, wielding a sword that appeared to be a natural extension of his arm.

Breanna had returned from the church to see her uncle, aunt, and several others gathered on one of the training fields outside the castle gates. Curious, she'd wandered over, only to discover that Gabriel had begun working with Savaric's men. Indeed, Savaric had bid Alfred join them, and the man had sped off to collect his training sword.

Breanna watched as Gabriel put the men through a series of moves. Using both hands on the sword or only one, they lunged and faded, pivoted and sliced, retreated and advanced. The air sang as both steel and wooden blades sliced through it.

The way Gabriel moved made Savaric's men appear clumsy. Breanna had never witnessed a display of lethal strength and skill executed with such grace. "He's remarkable," she murmured, her heart quickening.

"He certainly makes it look easy," Linette said, leaning on her husband's good arm.

His injured arm safely ensconced in a sling, Savaric

gave a nod of agreement. "Because he wields in God's name."

"Aye," Walter said. "It makes a difference."

Savaric regarded him. "Were you ever that good?"

"Not quite." Walter's mouth quirked as he folded his arms. "Close, though."

Savaric grunted. "He's a merciless teacher. He's got my squire wearing full battle kit and cleaning out the hay loft."

"Excellent," Walter replied. "It'll build the lad's strength."

"It'll hopefully take him down a peg or two," Savaric said. "I saw the bruises on the orphan boy's body today. I'd better not see any more."

The conversation saddened Breanna. She felt ashamed that they'd all missed Flip's abuse and promised herself she'd pay more attention to the boy from now on, following through with what Gabriel had started.

At that moment, Gabriel called a halt, sheathed his sword, and approached. A sheen of sweat gleamed on his forehead, and tendrils of damp dark hair clung to the side of his face, but his breathing showed no sign of being laboured.

"My ladies." He nodded his acknowledgment to Linette and Breanna and then spoke to Savaric. "The men have had enough for today, Lord de Sable. I'll increase the length and intensity of the sessions as we continue. For now, they should eat and then rest awhile. I'll see them out here at dawn tomorrow."

"I warrant they can hardly wait," Savaric said, with

a nod. "I'm impressed. Nice work, Templar."

"They're already skilled swordsmen, my lord. I'm simply refining those skills a little." A small muscle ticked in his jaw as he regarded Breanna. "How is Father Dunstan today, my lady?"

"He is healing, sir, thank you," she replied, struggling to keep a blush from her cheeks. "If he feels well enough, he said he'll visit Ghyllhead tomorrow."

"Which reminds me," Savaric said, "I need to complete the report for Lord de Clifford while the details are fresh in people's minds. Do you still wish to write it, Breanna, or shall I ask the priest?"

"I'll do it," she replied. "I'll start this afternoon."

"If you'll excuse me," Gabriel said, acknowledging those around him with glance, "I need to make sure the hayloft has been cleaned properly."

Savaric laughed. "I do believe you're enjoying the poor lad's suffering."

Gabriel gave a tight smile. "You're mistaken, Lord de Sable. I take no pleasure in it at all."

"He's solemn to the point of austere," Linette said, watching as Gabriel strode away. "I find him to be a little self-righteous."

"Oh, I do not find him so, my lady." Breanna gave Linette a cold glance. "He is a humble man and goodhearted."

Linette chuckled and waved a hand. "Yes, I've noticed the way you look at him, Breanna. *Besotted* is the word that comes to mind. I'd find your obsession with him rather sweet if it wasn't for the fact that he's a monk."

A flush of heat spread across Breanna's face. "I am grateful to him is all, and rightly so, given what he's done for me."

"Ladies!" Smiling, Walter regarded Linette and then Breanna. "I do believe I smell roast chicken. May I escort you both to the great hall for the midday repast? With my lord's permission, of course."

"Granted," Savaric said, with a snort. "Saves me from banging their silly female heads together."

Afternoon sun slanted through the grey glass of the scriptorium, wrapping Breanna in its summer warmth. She settled onto the stool at the writing desk and picked up her quill. Then, as the sharpened nib hovered over the inkhorn, she went back in her mind to that terrible morning three days earlier.

Dear God, it seems longer than that.

Even so, the events played out effortlessly, with a level of recall that startled her. It felt as though she was there again, living through the terror.

Her wrist soon ached as, line-by-line, her report grew, and with it, her angst. Half-way through describing the moment when her abductor had pulled the ring from her finger, she set the quill down and glanced at her right hand.

The mark where her mother's ring had sat for the past few years could still be seen. Where was the ring now? Gracing the finger of some outlaw's wife or daughter, most likely.

Blinking away tears, she rubbed at her temple, picked up the quill, and continued, only to halt again as she recalled the episode with the horse. The sudden jolt, the horrible sensation of falling, the harsh impact.

The snap of a man's neck as he hit the ground.

Breanna's mouth went dry. She tasted the gag anew, as if the vile thing was still jammed between her teeth, and bile rose to the back of her throat. As for those eyes, the whites yellowed, staring at her from behind his steel mask… those she would never forget.

Dead eyes. Unseeing.

Shivering despite the sunlight, she set the quill down again, hugging herself as she drew breath. Maybe she should have Father Dunstan finish the report. Then again, he could not do so without her input, so it would make little difference. The demons still had to be faced.

At that moment, the door creaked open, startling her. She looked over to see Gabriel on the threshold, a saddle bag slung over one shoulder.

He'd made a brief appearance in the Great Hall at midday, helping himself to some chicken and bread, which he'd wrapped in a piece of muslin. Then he'd left. She assumed he'd gone to the stable to share his meal with Flip and resisted an urge to join them.

Now, he stood in partial shadow, the sun not quite reaching him, the white of his garb blurred due to the silly tears in her eyes. She was reminded of the first time she'd seen him, striding through the woods, the answer to a prayer. Soon he'd be gone from her life, his fine appearance, gentle voice, and kind manner forever committed to memory. An angel among her demons.

She almost laughed at her foolish thoughts.

"Am I disturbing you, my lady?" he asked.

"Nay, not at all." Her smile wobbled. "Your timing is perfect, actually."

Overwhelmed by a rush of emotion, she covered her face with her hands as if doing so might stop the tears. She'd have had more success trying to hold back the tide. Sobs, hard and painful, rose up in her throat like stones, demanding release, and she had no choice but to oblige.

A gentle hand settled on her head, the thumb caressing the skin on her temple.

"This was bound to happen, Breanna." Gabriel's voice, so close to her ear, sent a shiver down her spine. "I warrant you'll feel better after it."

Still she wept, while Gabriel stroked her hair. In a perfect world, she thought, he would have pulled her into his arms and held her.

"Y-you must think me w-weak," she said, drained of emotion at last.

"Not at all."

Sniffing, she dared to raise her head. "It all came back to me as I was writing the report. I relived it. Every horrid detail."

"And you will do so again, many times over." He lifted his hand from her hair and sat down on the adjacent stool. "When evil touches our lives," he continued, "it leaves a mark that is often difficult to erase. I've seen knights affected by things they have seen or done on the battlefield. The images and sounds stay with them long after the battle is over."

"What of you?" Breanna lifted her kirtle and wiped the dampness from her cheeks. "Do you have such an affliction?"

He shrugged. "I have memories I'd prefer not to have, but they're not as troublesome as they used to be."

Curiosity stirred. "From your time in the Holy Land?"

"Some, aye. Not all." Clearing his throat, he leaned forward and regarded her parchment. "You write beautifully, my lady"

It was, Breanna realized, a pointed and blatant change of subject, which only served to stoke her curiosity even more. Most of what she'd learned about Gabriel had come from Savaric who, as lord of Ghyllhead, had every right to question those who lived within his walls. But even he seemed to respect the Templar's penchant for privacy and knew little beyond where Gabriel had come from and where he was going.

"Thank you," she said. "I'm about finished. I've described everything up to the moment I escaped, and see little point in detailing anything beyond that. I assume you're here to write a letter?"

"I am." He bent to pick up the bag at his feet. "I find the noise in the great hall a little distracting and thought I'd take advantage of this place."

"I told you, you're welcome to use it anytime," she said. "I'm not sure how easy it will be to send a letter to Scotland, though, given the conflict between us."

A corner of his mouth lifted. "I never said where the letter was going, my lady."

"Ah." A touch of warmth came to her cheeks. "I...I just assumed that's where it would be going. Nay, that's not true." She wrinkled her nose. "I'm curious about you and I just wanted to know, that's all."

A twinkle came to his eyes. "Then you should have asked."

"But I get the feeling you don't like questions."

"It depends who's asking them." Tilting his head, he regarded her. "You can ask me anything you like. If I don't want to answer, I won't, but I'll not be offended by your asking."

Her eyes widened. "You won't?"

His eyes softened. "I doubt you could ever offend me, Breanna."

The admission made her heart sing, and she shifted on her seat. "So, will the letter be going to Scotland?"

For the first time in her presence, he laughed. "Aye," he said. "It'll be going to Scotland."

After that, Breanna shamelessly indulged her curiosity, and Gabriel, for the most part, indulged her. She asked about the places he'd been, learned he spent time in the Holy Land, Cyprus, and Egypt. He described the sacred sites, the pyramids, the desert storms, and even the wildlife to be found there. She learned he'd acquired much of his healing knowledge while garrisoned there and had even learned to speak passable Arabic. He refused, gently, to answer any questions about the battles he'd fought.

"Such talk is not meant for a woman's ears, my lady," he said.

She had not persisted, but instead asked, "And what of Scotland? How was it there?"

Gabriel's expression softened. "I had my doubts at first, being English, but I was made welcome. Treated as one of them.

He described, in startling detail, the castle that sat on a cliff overlooking the sea and a majestic landscape not so different from Cumberland. Then he spoke of his friend, Ewan, whose grandfather had also been a Templar, and of a church in a secret glen that offered a standing promise of safe-haven to any Templar knight who needed one.

"It sounds heavenly. Magical, even," Breanna said, heaving a sigh. "I must ask myself why you would wish to leave such a place. Do you not miss it?"

He looked startled for a moment. "I do, of course. But I understand that Furness Abbey is also a place of great beauty. And the abbot there is a good friend. Someone I've known since childhood."

"Ah, I see." Breanna pondered the similarities they'd shared as children—specifically being deprived of a mother at a young age. "How come your mother died so young? What was the cause?"

At that exact moment a cloud must have passed over the sun, for the room darkened. Gabriel looked at the window, his expression equally as shadowed.

"That is a question I cannot answer, my lady."

She blinked. "You don't remember?"

"I remember being told the cause of her death," he replied. "I just didn't believe it."

"Why not?"

As if trying to decide how to respond, Gabriel stared at her for a moment. Then he rose to his feet, letting the saddlebag fall to the floor.

"Another time perhaps," he said, frowning as he bent to retrieve his belongings, some of which had spilled onto the floor. "If you'll excuse me, my lady, I've been lax in my supplications of late. I need to remedy that."

Confused by Gabriel's sudden change of demeanor, Breanna also stood. "But you haven't written your letter yet."

"It can wait till tomorrow."

The abruptness of his tone made her stomach clench. "It seems I've managed to do what you said I could not, sir," she said. "I've offended you."

He picked up an errant quill and tucked it into his bag. "Nay, my lady, you have not offended me."

"But you seem flustered, for want a better word."

"I am never flus..." Gabriel drew breath as if collecting himself and looked at her with a grim smile. "You're a dangerous woman, Breanna Glendenning."

Breanna's eyes widened. "Should I ever be asked to describe my character, sir, dangerous is not a word I would think to choose."

"Nevertheless." He ran a hand through his hair. "'Tis true I'm a private man. I dislike trivial conversations. Unless I have something of worth to say, I prefer to remain silent, and frequently wish other people would do the same. Only God knows what lies in my heart and mind, because I've never been compelled to share all that I am with anyone else." A corner of his mouth lifted. "Until today."

Breanna frowned. Had she just been complimented? Or denounced? "It troubles you that I find you interesting?"

"Nay, my lady," he replied. "It troubles me that I find your interest pleasing."

"Oh!" A horde of butterflies took flight in her belly. "I… I don't know what to say."

"Then I would rather you say nothing." He hoisted the saddlebag over his shoulder. "Understand, Breanna, I'm obliged to resist and reject such feelings. I'm committing a sin simply by being alone with you, and such lapses must cease. Don't be offended, then, if I keep a certain distance from you in the days to come. I must also ask that you tolerate and respect it."

Breanna's horde of butterflies turned into a lump of clay. "But we've done nothing wrong."

"*You* have done nothing wrong," he said, moving past her. "The fault lies entirely with me."

"So, I cannot even speak to you?" Desperation elevated her voice. "You cannot ignore me completely, Gabriel. That would be unkind and… and ill-mannered."

He groaned and turned back to her with an anguished expression. "Of course you can speak to me," he said. "I *want* you to speak to me. But it cannot be like this anymore." He glanced about. "In isolated places where I am tempted to…"

Her heart quickened. "Tempted to what?"

His bold gaze swept over her, head to toe, and his jaw tightened. "To betray the trust your uncle has placed in me," he said, and then left the room without another pause.

Not sure whether to laugh or cry, Breanna continued to stare at the place where he'd stood moments before. She realized, of course, that her growing attraction to him was impractical. For her own sake, she should also resist and reject the feelings that had set her heart against her head. But, unlike Gabriel, she could never label those feelings as wrong.

"What I feel for you is not sinful, Gabriel," she whispered and dropped her gaze. "Never that."

And then she saw it.

A piece of fabric lay on the floor by her desk, partially unfolded. It looked to be small, square patch of linen, its edges yellowed and frayed. It was also face down, evident from the dozens of delicate silken knots tied off on the backside.

A piece of embroidery.

Frowning, Breanna picked it up, turned it over, and unfolded it onto her hand, her eyes widening as she did so. Never had she seen a piece of work so finely crafted, each tiny stitch perfectly sized and exquisitely placed. The jewelled colours had obviously faded somewhat, but were still striking. The circular pattern appeared to be a puzzle of some sort; a collection of fragments, each one a depiction on its own, joined together to create a singular image. When Breanna looked closely, she could make out the tiny likenesses of people—apostles, perhaps. Or saints. In any case, it was quite beautiful.

It had evidently been kept folded too, and for a long time, judging by the creases embedded the fabric. It could only belong to Gabriel and must have spilled onto the floor with his other belongings. She wondered about its significance, certain it must have one, and then shrugged her curiosity away. It was none of her concern. She'd return it to him and leave it at that.

A short while later, with everything tidied away, Breanna delivered the report to her uncle and then went in search of Gabriel.

She found him in the stable talking to Cedric, and she lingered on the threshold, waiting for an opportune moment to interrupt.

"You've worked hard," he was saying to the squire. "Take some time to refresh yourself, but be out at the training fields after the bell rings for Terce. Bring your wooden sword and shield. Where's Hubald?"

"Helping Flip stack the kitchen firewood," Cedric replied, his tone somewhat sulky.

Gabriel nodded. "When they come back, have them—" His eyes met Breanna's, narrowing as they did so. "Have them bring Kadar in from the paddock," he finished. "And tell Flip to wait here for me. I'll talk to him later."

Breanna pasted a smile on her face as he approached.

"My lady," he said, his expression guarded, "is something wrong?"

"Nothing at all." She held out the piece of fabric. "I'm sorry to trouble you, but I found this in the scriptorium and believe it might be yours."

Gabriel gave a soft gasp and took the piece of fabric from her outstretched hand. "Thank you." A look of tenderness came to his eyes. "I didn't realize I'd dropped it."

"You're welcome," she replied, losing her smile. "It appears to be something you have long treasured. It would be a pity, then, to lose it."

And with that, she spun on her heel and walked away.

"Wait, Breanna, please."

Gabriel's plea caused her stomach to clench as she looked back. "Yes?"

He approached. "Walk with me, my lady."

She frowned. "I thought you said—"

"I know what I said," he said, glancing about. "But we are not alone out here."

"Ah, yes." She feigned an incredulous look "That's right. I'm dangerous."

"I did not mean to offend you. Quite the opposite." He appeared to ponder. "Perhaps tempting is a better choice of word, the weakness being mine."

A pertinent reply poised itself on the tip of her tongue, but she bit it back and fell into step beside him. "May I know the history of that embroidery?"

she asked. "I have never seen anything so exquisite."

"My mother gave it to me before I went to foster. 'Tis all I have left of her. I don't even know where her body rests because my father refused to tell me."

Breanna gasped. "Oh, Gabriel. I'm so sorry."

"'Tis why I value it so highly." Gabriel looked down to where it rested in his hand. "And I'm breaking yet another Templar rule by keeping it."

Breanna blinked. "What rule?"

"The ownership of personal possessions," he replied, with a shrug. "It is forbidden to do so in most monastic houses."

"Yet you still have it."

"I have it now. I surrendered it when I first joined the Order, but asked the Master if it might be stored and kept rather than destroyed. Since the depiction is taken from a house of God, he agreed, and I managed to get it back before we went into exile."

"A house of God?"

He nodded. "'Tis an exact copy of the rose window of *Notre Dame de Paris*. My mother often spoke of it. When the sun shines through it, she would say, it fills the church with a thousand rainbows. And she was right, for I have since seen it for myself."

Envisioning such a sight, Breanna gasped. "Oh, I would love to see such a thing."

"Maybe you will, one day."

"I doubt it. I've only ever been as far south as Kendal and as far north as Carlisle, whereas you have seen half the world."

"The world is not all coloured glass and rainbows,

Breanna." His hand brushed against hers, accidently, judging by the startled way he reacted.

Accidental or not, the brief touch fired an exquisite tingle up Breanna's arm and across her scalp. She could only imagine what it would be like to be held by this man, to feel his caress and his kiss. To be so taken by someone, yet denied hope of ever being with him, seemed…

Breanna halted. "Unfair."

"What is?"

"This. Us." She grimaced. "You say I am a temptation and you cannot be alone with me. Yet that is your choice, not mine. You *choose* to pursue a monastic life, Gabriel, and I respect it. I even admire it. But, by making your choice, I am left with none. At least, where you're concerned."

His brow creased. "I have never misled you, Breanna. You've always known the direction of my path."

"That is true," she replied. "But if being alone with me is so dangerous to you, perhaps you ought to reconsider that path."

The skin around his eyes tightened. "You speak boldly, my lady."

There, Breanna. You've managed to offend him. Are you happy now?

A sigh of regret escaped her as she lowered her eyes and kicked at a pebble on the ground. "I'm afraid it has forever been a fault of mine. I did not mean—"

"And what you have failed to consider," he continued, his tone hard, "is that monastic life is generally free from carnal temptation. Once I reach Furness, I will no longer be tempted to veer from chosen my path, because you…"

A spear of pain lanced through her heart as she locked eyes with his. "Will not be there?"

A muscle ticked in his jaw. At that same moment, the church bell rang out with the first peal of Terce, severing the icy thread of tension between them.

"Correct." Gabriel swept an impassioned gaze over her. "You will not be there. If you'll excuse me, my lady, I'm due on the training field."

Chapter Ten

There were definite advantages, Gabriel decided, to being in a foul mood. For one thing, it increased his stamina two-fold, which meant the training session that evening lasted longer than planned. The physical demands helped purge his frustration somewhat. Those same demands, however, pushed Savaric's men to their knees and made young Cedric beg for mercy, but neither was of consequence to Gabriel. It was better than riding out and killing someone, which is what he'd initially felt like doing.

He released them from their torture at last and approached Savaric and Walter.

"'Tis the celibate lifestyle," Savaric said, as Gabriel slid his sword into its scabbard. "I guarantee your endurance would suffer if you had a woman in your bed every night. Maybe I should tell the men to curtail their tupping."

It took all Gabriel had not to respond with an acerbic remark.

"Aye, and good luck with that, my lord," Walter retorted. "You'd have a rebellion on your hands."

"I'll see them again at dawn, my lord," Gabriel said. "Unless you have any objections."

"None at all." Chuckling, Savaric nodded toward his men, who were all but crawling off the field. "They might, though."

Gabriel eyed Savaric's sling. "How is the arm?"

"Useless," Savaric replied. "Maybe I should persuade you to stay longer."

Not likely, Gabriel thought, wishing he hadn't even promised the man a fortnight. "Have someone fill up a small bag with barley and then sew it shut. Use it to exercise your hand by squeezing and releasing, like so." Gabriel mimicked the movement. "It'll help keep the arm limber, but do not overdo it. As the wound heals, I'll suggest some other ways to keep the muscles working."

The other advantage of his mood, Gabriel thought, as he headed for the stables, was that it had sharpened his mind, clearing it of all fanciful thoughts and sinful clutter. He intended to make sure it remained that way.

"Flip?" he called, shrugging of his mantle as he entered.

"Here, sir," the boy replied, peeking over the gate from inside Kadar's stall. "I fed Kadar and combed his mane again. He's well used to me now, I think."

"Good lad." Gabriel regarded the boy's grubby face. "How did things go today? Did you work hard?"

Flip nodded. "I stacked a pile of logs taller than myself, sir."

"Impressive." Gabriel continued to strip down to his waist. "And were you well treated?"

"Aye."

"How are the bruises?"

"I think they're nearly gone." Flip lifted up his shirt and squinted at his belly, which was even grubbier than his face. Gabriel made a mental note to have the boy properly bathed. The bruises, though still visible through the grime, had faded.

"Have you eaten?"

Tugging his shirt down, Flip nodded. "Lady Breanna brought me some cheese and bread and an apple. Oh, and a carrot for Kadar."

Gabriel paused at the mention of Breanna's name. "That was kind of her," he said, as much to himself as to the boy. "You've done well, little knave. I'm proud of you. There's an undershirt in that saddlebag. Get it for me, will you? And then come out of there. I don't want you getting under Kadar's hooves."

Gabriel wandered over to the water-butt and doused himself to rinse the sweat from his body. It also took some of the edge off his mood. Refreshed, both in body and mind, he took the shirt from Flip.

"My thanks," he said, tugging the shirt over his head. "Now go and get some rest. I'll see you in the morning."

Gabriel opened his eyes and stared up at the Great Hall's lofty ceiling, which was still steeped in darkness. The night, so far, had not been kind. Around him, the sounds of slumber continued from those fortunate enough to have attained sleep. He turned to look at the hour-candle, burning atop a table by the door. Still an hour or so till sunrise, it seemed. He sat up and ran a hand through his hair.

He couldn't shift the image of the pain he'd seen in Breanna's eyes when he'd made the comment about temptation. At the same time, he felt his response had been justified. Breanna's bold remarks had overstepped the bounds of discretion. Then again, some of what she'd said had merit. Perhaps he'd been a little harsh.

So much for a mind cleared of clutter. Gabriel gritted his teeth and shoved his blanket aside. The chapel beckoned.

He lit a candle, placed it atop the altar and then knelt. For a while, he merely gazed at the cross and the shadow it cast upon the wall, allowing his mind to empty of all impure thought. Then he bent his head and prayed for guidance.

Moments later, the chapel door creaked open, followed by the sound of light footfalls on the wooden floor. Gabriel lifted his head once more, anticipation quickening his heart. He knew who it was. He felt Breanna's presence as keenly as the morning sun on his face, and it shook him to the core.

She knelt beside him and he dared to glance over, regretting his decision a moment later, for the sight of her stole his breath. She wore a simple kirtle of blue that enhanced her sweet curves. Her hair hung in a loose braid over one shoulder, while soft, untamed tendrils framed a face softened by candlelight.

Breanna's innocence and purity shone from within. But, for Gabriel, she was also the epitome of temptation. She represented man's greatest weakness; a reminder of how easily a disciplined, celibate soul, when confronted by the such feminine grace, could stray from its chosen path. His body stirred and he didn't even try to fight it. Increasingly, whenever he found himself in her presence, he was lost. And, also increasingly, he found it nearly impossible to stay away from her.

She finished her prayer and crossed herself. "I'm so sorry, Gabriel" she whispered, without looking at him. "I had no right to speak to you that way. I couldn't sleep for thinking about how I offended you. Please forgive me."

"There is nothing to forgive." He rose to his feet and held out a hand. "Come with me, Breanna."

Without hesitation, she placed her hand in his, and wordlessly, he led her outside. A half-moon cast a tepid silver glow that did not quite expel the darkness. Gabriel kept hold of Breanna's hand as they descended the steps, only releasing it when they reached a quiet spot at the rear of the keep.

There, he set her opposite him so he could look at her face, which appeared ghostly in the low light. The compulsion to lower his lips to hers was close to overwhelming.

"I find it difficult to be anything but forthright," he said, "especially with those I respect. That is what I intend to be with you now."

"I would rather you were." Her chin lifted. "I know I'm deserving of your censure."

"Nay, you're deserving of the truth. You need to understand why I said what I said." Inhaling her soft scent, he searched for a way to begin, and decided to simply voice the thoughts in his head. "Do you have any idea what you do to me? How you make me feel?"

Her brows raised. "I… I believe you like me well enough," she replied. "I've seen it in your eyes. I see it even now."

"*Like* you well enough?" Gabriel gave a soft laugh. "In all my years as a Templar, no woman has made me question my chosen path. Not one. Till I met you. Yes, I like you well enough, Breanna, and therein lies my dilemma. You're my one temptation. My weakness. When I'm near you, I feel things I should not feel. I *want* things I should not want." His gaze wandered over her body. "Things forbidden to me. Things sinful to me. Your observations earlier today had merit. I spoke poorly, and for that, I apologize. I ask only that you be aware of how much you affect me because, despite that, my path remains the same and I will not deviate from it."

He waited, anticipating her response.

Worrying her lip, Breanna looked away. "I understand," she said, turning back to him, her eyes unreadable in the shadows. "Truly, I do. I appreciate your honesty, and shall pay heed to what you've said. May I still spend time with you while in the company of others, though?"

She might as well have reached into his chest and plucked out his heart.

"I would be saddened if you did not," he said.

"Then, all is well." Smiling, she glanced skyward. "I believe I felt a spot of rain. If you'll excuse me, sir, I shall take my leave of you. Perhaps we shall see each other at breakfast?" Noiselessly, she turned and disappeared into the night. Gabriel looked to the heavens, where not a single cloud drifted. He stayed where he was till the sun rose.

Chapter Eleven

The three horsemen appeared mid-morning of the next day, approached the gates of Ghyllhead, reining in their horses at the edge of the training field. Gabriel called a halt to his training and looked to Savaric, who waved him over.

"'Tis the Baron de Clifford." Breathing hard, Alfred shook the sweat from his hair. "Lord Warden of the Marches. He'll be here about the attack."

Gabriel nodded his understanding. "Continue without me," he said, sheathing his sword as he wandered over to where Savaric stood with Walter. Linette had also been present for a short while before a rain-shower had chased her indoors. Breanna had been absent for the past two mornings. In fact, Gabriel had seen little of her at all since their moonlit exchange. He told himself it was a good thing, and then wondered why he found himself looking for her always, and why he felt such disappointment when she failed to appear.

When he *had* seen her, she'd been as amiable as ever, blessing him with a greeting and one of her sweet smiles. She continued to look tired, however, which troubled him.

"Templar," Savaric bellowed, as Gabriel drew near, "this is Baron Robert de Clifford, Lord Warden of the Marches. Lord de Clifford, this is Gabriel Fitzalan, the knight responsible for bringing my niece safely home."

Robert de Clifford could not have been much older

than Gabriel and stood equally as tall, but with limbs as gangly as a youth. An orderly crop of mouse-brown hair hung almost to his shoulders, matching the neatly clipped beard that added sharpness to his already-narrow jaw. His eyes, beset by heavy brows, regarded Gabriel with unabashed interest. "Your presence at Ghyllhead has not gone unnoticed, Templar. I cannot decide if you're brave or foolish for continuing to wear that garb."

"I consider myself neither, Lord de Clifford. I wear it because I vowed to do so, and will continued to do so till I leave the order."

"Which, I understand, will be when you get to Furness in a few days."

"God willing, aye."

"Hmm." De Clifford gestured to the men on the field. "I was watching as we rode up and liked what I saw. I agree with Savaric. 'Tis a pity to put down such a skilled sword. You should reconsider."

Gabriel kept his expression impartial. "I have already given it much consideration, my lord. My decision is made."

"He'll not be swayed, de Clifford. Believe me, I've tried." Savaric gestured to the field and addressed Gabriel. "Finish here, then join us in the Great Hall."

"As you wish," Gabriel replied, frowning, "though I'm not sure I have anything of worth to offer."

"You were the first to witness to Lady Breanna's condition subsequent to her escape," de Clifford said, soberly. "I wish to hear those details."

Gabriel stepped into the hall a short time later.

Savaric, De Clifford, and De Clifford's men sat at a quiet table in the corner. Breanna was there too, seated next to Father Dunstan. They kept a respectful silence as Lord de Clifford cast his eyes over the parchment in his hands. Other similar scrolls sat on the table before him—additional reports undoubtedly.

Gabriel slid quietly into a seat opposite Breanna. Their eyes met and she gave him a quick smile before turning her attention back to De Clifford. Fatigue showed itself in the pallor of her skin and the shadows beneath her eyes. Her nerves, too, were frayed, judging by the way her fingers locked and unlocked themselves atop the table. Gabriel wanted to reach out and cover her hands with his, to calm their skittish dance.

Father Dunstan nodded a silent greeting to him. Much of the priest's bruising had faded, though enough evidence of his injuries remained.

"I commend you, Lady Breanna." De Clifford, his expression grave, set the parchment down. "A concise and detailed account of your abduction. It is also a disturbing read, and must have taken courage to write. I find it interesting, too, that you believe the man to have been high-born."

"Why interesting?" Savaric asked. "Do you have suspicions about who he might be?"

"Not specifically, but if he was of noble birth, his death might make him easier to identity. Someone, somewhere, is missing a son or a brother or even a husband. If so, I'll hear about it. I have many sets of eyes and ears working for me."

"I fail to understand why such a man would choose to run with outlaws," Breanna said.

"'Tis not so uncommon, my lady," De Clifford replied. "There are those among us who readily abuse their position and power. I see similarities between this incident and several others in the area, which leads me to believe there might be a connection. You were fortunate, in this case, to have escaped largely unscathed. Others did not fare as well."

"Yes," Breanna replied, dropping her fidgeting hands into her lap, "I was very fortunate." Again, her eyes briefly met Gabriel's before she lowered them. He felt what had become a familiar tug at his heart.

"That said, I would like hear from the man who came to your aid." De Clifford leaned forward and regarded Gabriel. "Tell us, Templar, how you found the lady and in what condition you found her."

Gabriel cleared his throat and relayed the details of that day. A murmur of amused disbelief arose among De Clifford's men when they heard about Theo's involvement. Gabriel kept his eyes on Breanna as he spoke, watching for signs of distress as his account continued. She held his gaze too, as if taking strength from the support it was meant to convey. If anything, her previous angst seemed to subside as he continued to speak, much to his gratification.

"The lady's endurance is admirable," Gabriel said, in the end. "As is her courage."

"Indeed." De Clifford's mouth twitched. "And I should like to meet this fox one day. I confess I have never heard the like."

"I consider him a friend," Breanna said, a smile appearing at last.

"He's a mangy cur, my lord," Savaric said, giving Breanna a fond glance.

"Who deserves more credit than I for returning your niece safely to Ghyllhead," Gabriel replied.

De Clifford looked at Father Dunstan. "Are you sure there's nothing you care to add, Father?"

The priest shook his head. "As I said, my assailant did not speak, and his face was covered. I cannot think of anything that might help with your investigation."

"And the men you found in the woods that same day, Savaric. You're certain they were not part of this group?"

"Near certain, my lord," Savaric replied. "They were forest rats. Five of them. Two of them were wounded, one quite badly. I'd be surprised if he survived."

De Clifford grunted. "I'll cast out some nets and see what we haul in, but for now, it would seem we're done here." He gathered up the papers and rose to his feet. "I can assure you that the investigation has already begun, Savaric. I shall keep you informed as to my findings."

"I would appreciate it," Savaric said, finding his feet also. "But you need not leave yet, my lord. You're welcome to stay for the midday repast."

The man shook his head. "Another time, perhaps."

Savaric looked mildly disappointed. "Then I shall see you out."

"May I accompany Father Dunstan back to St Bega's after the repast, Uncle?" Breanna asked. "'Tis the Sabbath tomorrow and I'd like to take some flowers for the altar."

Father Dunstan chuckled. "And I'm sure Theo will be happy to see you as well."

Breanna shook her head. "Nay, Theo is not the reason…" A touch of colour came to her cheeks. "Well, maybe he's *part* of the reason I'd like to go."

Father Dunstan chuckled again. "It's quite all right, child. I'm happy to provide you with the means to see him. Besides, I enjoy your visits and your gifts."

"Aye, you may." Savaric threw a glance at Gabriel. "Escort her, will you, Templar?"

Breanna gave a soft gasp. "Oh, nay. I'll ask Alfred."

"Why Alfred?" Savaric gave Gabriel a questioning glance. "Are you busy this afternoon?"

He couldn't lie, but proffered an excuse. "Nay, my lord, though I have yet to change your bandages."

Savaric waved a dismissive hand. "They can wait till later," he said, and followed De Clifford out of the hall.

"By all the saints, Gabriel, I didn't think." Breanna grimaced. "I'll ask Alfred anyway."

"Nay, you will not." Gabriel shrugged. "I shall enjoy seeing Theo as well."

"Is something amiss?" Frowning, Father Dunstan looked from one to the other. Then his brow cleared. "Ah, your vows. Of course. But you should have told Savaric the truth, Gabriel. He'd have likely complained, but he'd respect your reasons."

"Savaric trusts me to protect that which he loves, Father," Gabriel said, "and I will do as he asks."

It had been nine days since the attack, since Breanna had first laid eyes on Gabriel. It felt so much longer than that, yet looking ahead, the four days remaining till his departure seemed poised to fly like the wind.

It would be a relief, she told herself, stealing a look at him as she arranged a freshly-picked bunch of daisies in the vase atop the altar. He stood in a patch of sunlight listening, at last, to Father Dunstan's tale of St Bega, to whom the church had been dedicated.

For the first time in her life, Breanna had come to understand the real meaning of want. It went way past a desire to eat or drink or sleep. It wasn't love, she decided. It was a promise of love destined to remain unfulfilled. A cruel reality that left her *wanting*. Part of her wished she'd never met Gabriel, mostly because she knew his leaving wouldn't be a relief at all.

It would break her heart.

Heaving a sigh, she stepped back and admired her handiwork. "What do you think, Theo?"

The fox, who had been sitting, rose to all fours and flicked his bushy tail.

"Very nice, my dear," Father Dunstan said, approaching. "Thank you."

"You're welcome, Father. They are pretty, aren't they? They're one of my favourite flowers."

Gabriel now stood in shadow several steps away, watching.

"Shall we go?" Breanna asked him.

"Whenever you're ready, my lady."

They stepped out to cloudy skies and warm air sharpened by the tang of the sea—a sure sign of rain. Breanna picked up her skirts as they wandered back up the lane. "Did you enjoy the tale of our saint?"

"I did."

"There is a convent dedicated to her also." Breanna shaded her eyes and looked toward the west. "Like your Scottish castle, it sits on the coast overlooking the sea. On clear days, you can see the Isle of Man from there."

"Yes, Father Dunstan mentioned it."

"Ah."

"How old is he?"

Breanna's brow lifted. "Father Dunstan? I'm not certain. Quite old, I should think."

Chuckling, Gabriel shook his head. "Nay, I meant Theo."

"Oh!" She laughed. "This is his second summer, so he's still young, but his kingdom is a dangerous place. I know there'll be a day, probably sooner than later, when he'll not be here to greet me."

"Ah, but he's clever." Gabriel paused and crouched to pet the fox. "I wouldn't be surprised if he's around for many years yet."

"I pray you are right, sir," she replied. "I would

miss him."

They were being so polite, Breanna thought, both of them dancing around the forbidden boundaries of intimacy and even the fringe of friendship. She hated it. It felt foreign to her. Uncomfortable. Akin to having her shoes on the wrong feet.

"I will miss you, Gabriel," she blurted out, feeling at once better and then immediately worse.

He straightened. "Breanna—"

"Nay, you don't have to reply. You don't have to say anything at all." She waved a nonchalant hand and walked on. "I just wanted you to know that."

He moved to catch up with her. "I'll miss you too, Breanna."

"You will?"

"Of course. I told you how you make me feel. I'm not likely to forget all that the moment I leave."

Breanna heaved a sigh. "I wasn't sure how to respond to you the other night. I was tired and upset."

"I know."

"I lied about the raindrop."

"I know that too." His lip twitched. "There wasn't a cloud in the sky."

"So, if I promise not to tempt you into sin, can we maybe just enjoy what time we have left without being… uncomfortable?"

"I thought we'd already agreed to that," he said, "but you shouldn't make promises you cannot keep. Whenever you're near me, I'm tempted. 'Tis up to me to resist you."

She might have chosen a solemn reply, one that

better reflected the sad truth of her feelings. Instead, she chose frivolity. "Then I promise not to lure you into dark corners, Templar."

Chapter Twelve

Late afternoon sun tumbled through the scriptorium window. Gabriel breathed softly as he put quill to parchment, inking the words that would soon, God willing, find their way to Scotland without obstacle. No doubt his friends would be waiting for word of his progress. He'd been at Ghyllhead for ten days already. Enough of a delay.

That morning, the Sabbath, he'd received the Holy Eucharist at St Bega's, after which he had spent a quiet time at prayer in Ghyllhead's private chapel. Breanna had joined him there for a while, kneeling in silence at his side. She looked more rested, her grey eyes brighter, cheeks bearing a sweet touch of colour.

Later, he'd attended Savaric's wound, which was healing better than he could have hoped. After that, he'd enjoyed the Sunday repast with the people of Ghyllhead, an event that brought to mind the ambience of Castle Cathan. And that, in turn, had reminded him that he had a letter to write.

So far, it had been a good day.

A sound from the doorway drew his attention, and he looked up to see Linette, whose face brightened at the sight of him. She stepped into the room and closed the door behind her. It seemed to be a calculated move, one that puzzled him.

"My lady." He set his quill down. "Is everything all right?"

She gave him a radiant smile. "Everything is fine, Gabriel. I'm simply surprised to find you here alone.

Where is Breanna?"

"I have no idea, my lady."

"I find that hard to believe." Fingering a small gold cross at her throat, she wandered over. "The girl is usually trailing at your heels is she not?"

"Nay, my lady." Uneasiness, in a mild form, played on Gabriel's composure. "Not usually."

A shaped brow lifted. "Oh? Then maybe my eyes have been deceiving me. In any case, 'tis obvious she is taken with you and you with her." A slender, manicured hand caressed the curve of her hip, as if to smooth a crease from her burgundy robe. It also seemed to be a calculated move, blatantly sensuous. "You cannot deny that, sir, surely."

Gabriel frowned. "May I know the reason for your visit, my lady?"

"My *visit*?" She laughed and glanced about. "Ghyllhead is my home, Sir Gabriel. I come and go as I please. 'Tis you the visitor here. Not I."

He summoned up a smile. "You are right, of course. Please forgive me. I'll take my leave of you."

Tutting, she moved closer. "No need for that." She peered at the parchment. "What are you writing?"

Gabriel resisted an urge to step back. "A letter, my lady."

"I can understand it, of course."

"Understand it?"

"My niece's obsession with you." The turquoise-blue of Linette's eyes glittered as she gazed up at him. "You did rescue her from a terrible situation after all, and…" she trailed a fingertip down the centre of his chest and then splayed her fingers over his heart, "you are more than pleasing to look upon. But I cannot quite fathom your interest in her. Why, she's little more than a child."

Gabriel suppressed a sigh, wrapped his fingers around her wrist, and lifted her hand away. "You're forgetting yourself, my lady."

A flush came to her cheeks as she tugged her wrist free. "As are you, sir. How dare you put your hands on me!"

"I was obliged to do so," Gabriel said, keeping his voice calm. "Perhaps you need reminding of what I am."

She scoffed. "What you are hasn't stopped you from fawning over that wayward niece of mine."

"It seems you have misunderstood, my lady. Breanna understands what I am."

"Pah! I doubt she cares. Her mother was a flagrant woman, and I fear Breanna is treading the same path. Savaric doesn't see it, of course. Or he turns a blind eye to it. I'm not sure which." She rubbed her wrist where he'd held her. "And you hurt me."

He bit down. "I did not intend—"

"I'll be bruised." A smirk appeared. "I guarantee it."

Gabriel gave her a look of genuine pity and bent to gather up his things. "I think it best I leave."

"Nay, please, finish your letter. I'm leaving." The smirk stayed, accompanied by a spark of malice in her eyes as she rubbed her wrist again. "But you'll regret this, I promise."

I already do. Gabriel swept his gaze over her. "I suggest you be careful with your threats, Lady de Sable."

She gasped "Are you threatening *me*?"

"Not at all," he replied. "Again, you misunderstand. Your husband is a good man and this, I fear, will hurt him."

A glimmer of what looked like shame flared in her turquoise eyes before the malice returned. "You accuse me of forgetting myself," she said, "yet I find it telling that you did not once deny your attraction to my niece. Perhaps you need to remind *yourself*, Templar, of what you are. Perhaps, for her sake, it is time you went on your way."

With undisguised contempt, she looked him up and down, and then fled the chamber.

Gabriel stared at the unfinished letter for a few moments. He saw no point in completing it. Not here. Not now.

His stay at Ghyllhead was at an end.

A short while later, Gabriel sat atop a stool in the armory and ran the whetstone along the edge of his blade. The exercise brought back memories of Ewan and their final night in La Rochelle eight months earlier. It had been a Wednesday, the eleventh day in the month of October. Ewan had been sharpening his sword, much as Gabriel was now doing.

The window had been open, he recalled. The night

had been unseasonably warm, like an afterthought of summer, and a cricket had been chirping. Yet, despite the perceived tranquility, a vague sense of foreboding soured the air.

Then Jacques returned from a meeting with the Master with news that would forever change their lives. He told them of King Philippe's intent to have the Templars arrested in a countrywide sweep two days hence, on Friday, the thirteenth day of October— a date Gabriel would never forget. They were told to leave without delay. To *retreat*, may God help them.

By the time the persecution began, Gabriel was aboard a ship, with his Templar brothers, on their way to Scotland.

Now, on this summer evening in England, with sunlight waning and birds singing, Gabriel was waiting for Savaric. He suspected he wouldn't have to wait too long, though he wasn't quite sure what to expect from the lord of Ghyllhead. He felt no fear, however. He'd done nothing wrong. Nay, he felt only sympathy for an unhappy woman and her husband, who had, undoubtedly, been misinformed.

A shadow fell across the doorway.

No, he hadn't had to wait too long at all.

"On your feet, Templar." Savaric de Sable stood, legs braced apart, on the threshold, his hand resting on the hilt of his sword. The sun at his back turned his rigid form into a solid, black shape.

Gabriel set the whetstone aside and rose, sword in hand. "My lord."

Savaric stepped forward, eyes narrowing at the

unsheathed sword. "You know why I'm here." It was not a question.

"I do." Gabriel slid the sword into its scabbard. "And I regret the reason for it."

The man's nostril's flared as he stepped closer. "You admit to it, then."

"That depends. To what are you referring?"

Savaric showed his teeth. "That you put your hands on my wife!"

"I do not deny that, my lord."

Savaric flinched. "Jesus Christ," he muttered, his hand falling to his sword hilt. "She said you'd deny it."

Gabriel's gaze didn't waver. "Then I fear the lady misjudged me, Lord de Sable."

Savaric shifted on his feet. "Have I misjudged you, Gabriel?"

"You must decide that for yourself," Gabriel replied, "but I pray your loyalty will be to your wife."

A glimmer of comprehension flickered in Savaric's eyes. "You realize you can no longer remain here," he said, looking as though he just swallowed vinegar.

"I do."

"You must be gone by morning."

Gabriel inclined his head. "As you wish, my lord."

Chest heaving, Savaric stared at him for a moment longer. "Jesus Christ," he muttered again, and then turned to walk away.

Trying to ignore the hollow feeling beneath his ribs, Gabriel headed for the stables. Leaving Ghyllhead had always been anticipated, of course, but he regretted the unpleasant terms of it. How quickly things could change. And how easily. He'd be sleeping with Kadar that night. The door to the keep was, at least in his mind, now closed to him.

Kadar rumbled a low greeting at the sight of his master. Gabriel heaved a sigh and rubbed the gelding's soft nose. Horses, he understood, but the wiles of women were beyond him. He couldn't even begin to fathom Linette de Sable's rationale. Had it simply been a ploy to get rid of him? If so, it made little sense, since he'd have been leaving in a few days anyway. As for his attraction to Breanna—true, he had not denied it, nor would he. But he'd faced and dealt with it. Hadn't he?

A scuffle from above caught his attention.

"Did you get a day off today, Flip?" he asked, without lifting his head.

"Mostly, sir." Another scuffle. "Does having a bath count as work?"

Gabriel looked up. "You had a bath?"

"Lady Breanna made me." He sniffed. "I smell funny now."

Gabriel smiled. "Clean, you mean."

"I s'pose."

"Come down here, little knave. I wish to speak to you."

Breanna must have taken a scrubbing brush to the lad, since he'd all but changed colour. His skin glowed, and his previously mousy hair now glinted with gold lights.

"You look much better," Gabriel said, giving the

boy's shoulder a gentle squeeze. "Still need some meat on your bones, though."

"Lady Breanna brought me some lamb today, sir," he replied, "with bread and an apple."

"I'm glad to hear it." Gabriel suppressed a sigh. "I'm leaving in the morning, Flip."

Flip's smile disappeared. "You are?"

"Aye."

His brow creased. "Are you coming back?"

When it came to children, Gabriel had always been somewhat ambivalent. They had never been part of his perceived future. A sudden unexpected wrench on his heart took him by surprise. He'd grown fond of this little lad, he realized. "Nay, I'm not coming back."

"But…" Still frowning, Flip looked at his hands, splaying his fingers as if calculating. "Has it been a fortnight already?"

"Not quite. I'm leaving earlier than planned."

"Why?"

"Because my time here is done, little knave." Gabriel touched the boy's cheek. "You don't have to worry about Cedric and Hubald, though. Lady Breanna will make sure they don't bother you anymore. And don't be afraid to tell her if they do, all right?"

Flip nodded.

Gabriel raised a brow. "Not acceptable."

The boy heaved an exaggerated sigh. "Yes, sir."

"Brother." Walter's voice drifted in from the doorway. "I would speak with you outside."

Gabriel nodded at Walter and then turned his attention back to Flip. "I'll be leaving early, and I'll need your help to get Kadar ready." He gave the boy's shoulder another squeeze as he moved past him. "So, go and get some rest."

"When Savaric told me, I didn't believe it," Walter said in hushed tones before Gabriel had even set foot outside the door. "But I heard what you said to young Flip just now. You're leaving."

"Aye."

"Why? Savaric wouldn't elaborate."

"It doesn't matter why. My time here is done, that's all."

Walter cocked his head. "Would it have anything to do with a lady, by any chance?"

Gabriel gave him a disapproving look. "Frivolous speculation does not become you, Brother."

He shrugged. "I've noticed the way Breanna looks at you and the way you look at her. Savaric was bound to see it eventually. Rescuing her from the forest wasn't enough for him to overlook it, I suppose."

Gabriel didn't try to correct him. "Does the lady know I'm leaving?"

"I don't think so. Not yet, anyway. Savaric had a face that would stop the tide and took himself off to his chamber with a flagon of wine." Walter gave a sober smile. "For what it's worth, I remember well the torture of female temptation."

"I would never have surrendered to it."

"Oh, I know that. I never surrendered to it either.

At least, not while I still wore the white. I'll be sorry to see you go, Brother. Watching you train Savaric's men has been a real pleasure." He held out a hand, and Gabriel took it.

"My thanks," Gabriel replied. "Your friendship has been appreciated."

"Likewise," Walter said. "And if I don't see you in the morning, Godspeed, Templar."

Gabriel awoke to grey light and a clatter of rain that sounded like glass beads hitting the stable roof. He sat up, brushed the straw from his hair, and rubbed a knot from his neck. He'd bedded down in Kadar's stall, but lain awake a good while before falling into an uneasy sleep. Stifling a yawn, he clambered to his feet.

"Time to go," he murmured, and ran a hand along Kadar's sleek back. "We've a long day ahead of us." The horse, his head drooping lazily, issued a low rumble from his chest.

Gabriel looked up at the hole in the hayloft floor. "Flip? Are you awake?"

No answer. He'd let the lad sleep a while longer, he decided, partly because he didn't relish dealing with another show of emotion.

He led Kadar from the stall and tethered him in readiness for tacking. The rattle of rain continued, and Gabriel glanced at the stable door, where a cascade of water tumbling from the roof had formed a silver curtain. If the foul weather continued, the day's journey promised to be worse than miserable. They'd be saturated before they'd even reached the castle gates.

As if thinking the same, Kadar turned and eyed his master, ears pricked in question. "We'll survive," Gabriel muttered as he settled the saddle on the horse's back and tightened the girth. The weather would not deter them. The misery of it would be a small price to pay. Gabriel yearned to be gone, to take back control of his heart and mind. Or at least, that's what he told himself.

Again, he glanced at the stable door, anticipating, wondering if Breanna had been told about his departure. The gloom within the stable matched his increasingly dark mood as he continued to ready Kadar. Saddle in place, he slid the bridle over the horse's head and fastened the cheek strap.

At that moment, a cloaked figure moved through the curtain of rain and halted just inside the door, panting as if winded. Gabriel cursed the sudden tightness in his chest and feigned interest in the stirrup leather. Dread replaced anticipation. Christ help him, he'd felt less angst confronting a horde of Mamluk warriors than having to face this slip of a girl.

"Gabriel." Breanna spoke his name on her exhale, her voice trembling a little.

He summoned the courage to look at her and she threw back her hood as their eyes met, hers wide and bright with emotion. Silver drops tumbled down the blue folds of her cloak to drip from her mud-spattered hem. A soft flush of pink stained her cheeks, and her chest rose and fell as she breathed through slightly-parted lips. Wayward strands of hair, dark and damp, formed tight ringlets that framed her face. Gabriel searched, but could find no guile in the image Breanna presented. Only truth and innocence.

God help me. How can such beauty be deemed sinful?

He inclined his head. "Breanna."

Her anxious gaze flicked briefly to Kadar, who stood tacked and near ready. "'Tis true then," she said, a slight waver in her voice. "When Flip told me you were leaving, I didn't believe him."

Gabriel cast a brief glance at the hole above Kadar's stall. "Flip told you?"

She nodded. "Yes."

"Where is he?"

"In the Great Hall. He refused to come with me. He says he doesn't want to say goodbye."

Gabriel winced. "Christ have mercy."

"Why did you not tell...?" Confusion and fear shadowed Breanna's expression. "I mean, may I know why you're leaving? It has not yet been a fortnight."

Gabriel bit down and gentled his voice. "I never intended to stay at Ghyllhead for long, my lady. You know that."

"Yes, but why now? Why today?" She moved closer. "Has something happened?"

He could not tell her the truth. "Nay."

"Then, I don't understand. My uncle is not yet fully recovered."

"He is much improved." Gabriel tugged the saddle

flap down. "I am not needed here any longer."

"But, I don't…" She faltered, her fingers tying themselves in knots as she glanced over her shoulder. "'Tis pouring, Gabriel, look! You cannot possibly leave in such weather."

No sooner had she uttered the words than the clattering downpour ceased, as if someone had plugged whatever hole had been open in the skies.

"Oh," she muttered, the small exclamation laden with disappointment.

Gabriel tightened his jaw and met her joyless gaze once more. "I've already stayed longer than planned," he said. "'Tis well past the time for me to go,

She gasped. "And you would have done so without a word of farewell to me? Please tell me that was not your intent."

"It was never my intent." He turned from her, picked up his saddlebags, and settled them over Kadar's rump. "But it might have been a consequence had you not come looking for me."

She fell silent for a moment. Then, "Something happened last night, didn't it? My uncle was in a terrible mood and refused to speak to anyone. Did you quarrel? Is that why you're leaving like this? Will you tell me?"

"There is nothing to tell, my lady."

"There has to be!" she cried, tears bright in her eyes. "This is all so sudden, Gabriel, and I fail to understand the urgency. There has to be a reason for it. After all we have shared, do I not deserve an explanation?"

Her plea found its mark and forced a sigh from him. "Yes, you do," he said, "but I have no wish to hurt you."

"So, you would leave without a word, believing it to be a painless solution?" A flush came to her cheeks. "I beg of you, Templar, do not spare me! I prefer the agony of truth to the torture of ambiguity."

Gabriel stifled a groan and turned to her. He had gazed upon her many times, finding both pleasure and fascination in her beauty. Ungilded by vanity or pride, it had a natural honesty about it.

He longed to touch her. Oh, he had done so a few times, but mostly due to necessity, such as when he'd come to her aid in the forest, or when he'd comforted her in the scriptorium. But he had never touched her as a man might touch a woman, with urgency and desire.

"God forgive me," he murmured.

Breanna's eyes widened slightly, but she remained still as Gabriel trailed his fingertips over the contours of her cheek, down the graceful line of her throat and across the exposed flesh of her chest. He halted his exploration at the neckline of her robe and placed his hand flat against her chest. It took all he had not to continue over the gentle rise of her breast and feel her respond to his touch, as he knew she would.

She responded anyway, lips parting as she inhaled, the rise of her nipple visible through the pale linen of her kirtle. Gabriel's body stirred in response. It was the first time he had touched her so intimately. And it would be the last.

The agony of truth.

He breathed in her essence and asked the question he had often pondered. "What is that scent you wear?"

She looked momentarily taken aback. "'Tis lily-of-the-valley. Mama used to wear it."

He almost laughed.

"Nay, I would not have left without a word, Breanna," he said. "I'd have waited here till you came to me, as I knew you would. As I *prayed* you would. And therein lies the truth of it. I cannot resist you. I must leave because I don't have the strength to remain. The temptations here are too great."

"So, you're leaving because of me." The blush remained on her cheeks as a spark of protest arose in her eyes. "Why can you not stay because of me?"

He groaned. "You once told me you believed there was a place for everything under Heaven. Theo has his place, you have yours, I have mine. And mine lies elsewhere."

Breanna gave her head a slight shake and glanced away for a moment. "I have never quite understood," she said, at last, "why the expression of love 'tween a man and a woman is deemed sinful."

"It is not sinful," Gabriel replied, "as long as it takes place within the sanctity of marriage. And since I'm sworn to celibacy, I cannot marry."

"But no one is forcing celibacy upon you, Gabriel. It is your choice, is it not? You could renounce your vows if you wished."

"That will not happen."

Her brows arched. "Never?"

He shook his head. "I am sworn to serve God. You know that. You have known it from the first moment we met."

"Yes, I have." A forced smile appeared accompanied by a fresh shimmer of tears. "But I... I have always hoped you might find a place for me in your heart as well."

Gabriel gave a half-shrug. "Even if I chose to renounce my vows, I could not marry you."

"Why not?"

"Because I have nothing of worth to bring to a marriage."

She huffed. "You speak of material worth, upon which I place little importance."

"But it is important to your guardian, who would see you well-matched. And rightly so." Gabriel unhooked Kadar's tether. "You're high-born. I'm a landless knight. The feelings we share are of little consequence to anyone but us."

"I know," she said, the expression on her face one of utter dejection. "It just seems so... unfair."

Gabriel parted with a sigh and gazed into eyes the colour of a stormy sky. "You must promise me something."

"What?"

"That you'll never leave Ghyllhead without an armed escort." His eyes narrowed. "Swear you will not."

A tear escaped and slid down her cheek. "Will I ever see you again?"

"Swear to me you will never—"

"Nay! I mean, yes, I swear it." Desperation edged her voice. "Gabriel, will I ever see you again?"

How could he answer such a question with any amount of certainty?

"If God wills it," he replied, his heart a solid thud in his ears. *It's time to go. Time to end this.* He grasped Kadar's reins and moved toward the doorway.

"Wait!" Breanna scurried after him. "Will you at least promise to send word when you arrive at the abbey? I would know that you are safe."

Gabriel stepped out into the bailey, where puddles of rain reflected the first hints of daylight. A few folks were bustling about. One or two even nodded a greeting, but most paid him little mind. They would not know of his imminent departure, which suited his preference for anonymity.

Unbidden, his mind slid back several weeks to the morning he'd left Castle Cathan. Then, his departure had been quite different, with a line of pale faces wearing brave smiles, a sharing of sentiment, a chorus of wishes for a safe journey.

And those cursed tears in Ewan's eyes.

A sudden sense of yearning caught Gabriel by surprise. He missed his friends deeply, he realized. All of them. He raised his gaze to the sky and snatched a lungful of damp air.

"Gabriel?"

Breanna's voice. By all things sacred, he would miss that too.

"I should have held you," he said, without looking

at her. "That day in the scriptorium, when you were crying? I should have held you." Cursing the lump in his throat, he tossed the reins over Kadar's neck, stuck his foot in the stirrup, and swung into the saddle. "I'll send word when I get to the abbey."

Before she had time to respond, Gabriel pressed his heels to Kadar's belly and urged the horse forward. He did not look back. He could not. To do so would engrave a memory on his mind that he would never wish to recall.

As he approached the gates, he glanced up at the gatehouse with a silent request, one answered moments later by the clanking rise of the portcullis. It had not even risen halfway before a shout echoed across the bailey.

"Hold!"

The gate ground to a halt, and Gabriel cursed under his breath. He twisted in the saddle to see Savaric striding across the bailey.

What now?

The lord of Ghyllhead appeared unkempt, as if he'd slept in his clothes, or just rolled out of bed and dressed hastily. He approached, set his hand on Kadar's bridle, and looked at Gabriel through bleary eyes.

Gabriel returned the man's gaze and waited.

"Before you go, Templar," Savaric said, sounding breathless, "there is something I wish to make clear."

Gabriel kept his expression passive. "Which is?"

"If I believed…" Savaric grimaced and ran a hand through his hair. "Ah, Christ help me. If I *suspected*, even in the smallest way, that you had done what my wife accused you of doing, you would not be leaving Ghyllhead this morning. Do you understand me?"

Gabriel gave a sober smile. "I do, my lord."

Savaric nodded and stepped back. "Godspeed, my friend," he said, signalling the gatehouse. The sluggish rattle of the portcullis' ascent commenced once more. Gabriel should have urged Kadar on without a backward glance, but before he could stop himself, he glanced over his shoulder.

And confronted the memory he'd tried to avoid.

Breanna stood where he'd left her, silent and watching, the blue of her cloak as bright as a jewel in the sombre dawn light. He was no longer close enough to see the tears on her cheeks, but he knew she wept.

You do have a place in my heart, Breanna. You've had it since the first time I saw you. And you will always have it.

A sudden, mad urge gripped him, demanding he remain at Ghyllhead and beg for Breanna's hand. Perhaps if he declared his fealty, offered his services as marshal, maybe Savaric might—

"My niece thinks she's in love with you." Savaric's voice shattered Gabriel's outlandish vision. "A foolish infatuation that will soon pass. Besides, she's to be wed by summer's end."

Wed?

Gabriel's hands tightened on the reins as he dragged his gaze back to Savaric. "Does she know?"

"Nay. The contract has yet to be signed. 'Tis a mere

formality, however."

At that same moment, the rattle of the portcullis ceased and the way to Gabriel's future stood open.

"I shall pray for her," he said, swallowing bile. Then, without another glance back, he urged Kadar onwards.

Once clear of the gates, Gabriel spurred the horse into a canter, eager to put distance between himself and Ghyllhead. But regret, and another deeper emotion he couldn't quite identify, travelled with him.

Wed? To think of Breanna with a man, to imagine him touching her... *loving* her, all but set his blood boiling.

"Cease," he said, through gritted teeth. "You will cease this now. What's done is done. You have played your part. She is not meant for you. Your path leads elsewhere."

With no small effort, he shifted his thoughts away from the past and forced himself to look forward. Two, maybe three days of travel, God willing, he would at last arrive at his intended destination. Furness Abbey. One of the most powerful abbeys in the land. Once there, he would surely find the peace he sought. An existence free from distraction and temptation.

He filled his lungs and began to recite the Apostles' Creed, whispering against the breeze. Lost in his supplication, he didn't see the fox standing in the middle of the road until he was almost upon it. Uttering a curse worthy of a less godly man, Gabriel tugged Kadar to a halt.

Theo?

As if in response, the fox yipped once, gave his tail a single wag, and turned a circle. Gabriel scowled at the creature. "Move aside," he said, nudging Kadar into a walk. Theo didn't move, forcing Gabriel to steer around him. The fox responded by scampering down the road and planting himself in the centre of it once more. Had the wily little vagabond been blessed with the power of speech, Gabriel knew it would have uttered one word.

Stay.

"Nay, you're wasting your time," Gabriel said, as he steered Kadar around the fox once more. "Be off with you."

But the creature ran ahead and repeated his performance. Both irritated and touched by the creature's persistence, Gabriel uttered a soft curse, reined in, and dismounted. Without hesitation, the fox trotted over. Gabriel crouched and stared into a pair of hopeful, amber eyes.

"I cannot stay, Theo, this is not my place. But keep watch over Breanna, all right?" Heaving a sigh, he scratched the fox behind the ear and then rose to his feet. "Would that we all had friends as loyal as you," he murmured, and nodded toward the hedgerow. "Now begone. And stay away from those dogs."

Ears drooping, Theo gazed at Gabriel for a moment longer. Then he backed up a step, turned, and disappeared into the undergrowth. The creature's disappointment was beyond dispute, and guilt ripped a hole in Gabriel's conscience. Even Kadar twisted his great head around and gave his master an accusing glance.

"'Tis a fox," Gabriel mumbled as he clambered back into the saddle. "Just a fox."

Nightfall found Gabriel dismounting outside the doorway of a roadside hostelry near the town of Kendal. Had the stars been visible, he'd have been content to spend the night beneath them, but they lay hidden behind a persistent layer of clouds. It had been a wearisome day of travel—much of it spent drying out between showers of rain. In truth, Gabriel sought sustenance for Kadar more than for himself. The horse deserved a decent feed and a dry bed.

A cross, carved into the capstone atop the hostelry doorway, further prompted Gabriel to enquire within.

He tethered Kadar and pushed the door open, nostrils flaring as he stepped into an airborne stew of smoke, unwashed bodies, and kitchen odours.

Aware of the sudden lull in conversation, Gabriel cast a gaze over the dark recesses of the interior. A diverse assortment of faces, their features lit by candleflame and lantern-light, appeared to be scrutinizing him with undisguised interest. Moments later, a sallow-complexioned man wearing the brown robes of a lay monk stepped out of the shadows. He also scrutinized Gabriel, but with something akin to apprehension. "Good eve, sir knight."

"Good eve, Brother," Gabriel replied. "I seek

shelter for myself and stabling for my horse."

"Of course." The man cleared his throat and shifted on his feet. "Um, I've little room to spare within, but you're welcome to bed down in the stable with your horse, if you wish. The stable lad will help you with your armor, unless you intend to sleep in it."

So, a second night in a stable. Well, it had been good enough for the infant Christ, Gabriel thought, and nodded his assent. "My thanks."

"And there's bread and ale on the table yonder. Take what you need."

Gabriel nodded again and cast a second glance around the room, this one challenging. The faces, most of them anyway, turned back to their food and conversation.

But some did not. In particular, a group of several men who eyed Gabriel with blatant animosity, as if assessing him.

"I'm sure they mean no harm," the monk said, obviously noticing the exchange. "The rumours about your order have likely stirred their curiosity."

"The rumours are just that," Gabriel replied. "Naught but hearsay."

"That may be." Grimacing, the man lowered his voice. "Nevertheless, you place yourself at risk wearing that mantle."

Gabriel raised a brow. "If they mean no harm, then I have naught to fear."

"I didn't mean here, although…" The man regarded the group of men, who had now turned back to their food. "I cannot vouch for all beneath this roof. There may be those who believe the accusations you face."

"The accusations are false, and I will not..." Gabriel drew a breath to calm his rising annoyance. "No matter. I have no wish to cause you any trouble, Brother. I'll be gone before dawn."

"And may God go with you." The man crossed himself. "These are dangerous times."

Sleep came that night, turbulent in nature, with fragmented dreams that flowed through Gabriel's mind like a rain-swollen stream. It carried with it reflections of familiar faces, some living, some dead, their mouths shaping words he could not hear.

Except for Breanna's words. Those he heard, over and over.

'Will I ever see you again?'

'If God wills it.'

Gabriel opened his eyes to darkness, hard with desire for a woman he could never have. He wondered if she lay awake too, thinking of him as he thought of her. Then, from somewhere nearby, came the rustle of hay and the deep mumble of a man's voice, followed by a soft, feminine moan. It seemed others had bedded down in the stable as well. And they were not sleeping, either.

Christ have mercy.

Gabriel closed his eyes and attempted to close his ears, but the prayers uttered in his mind did not deafen him to the lustful sounds of pleasure. The episode, fortunately, was over quickly, culminating in a singular cry from the woman and a guttural groan from the man.

But it left Gabriel in a tortured state. Only that morning, he had stood in another stable and dared to touch Breanna. He recalled her swift intake of breath. The way her skin felt—softer than any silk. She'd stood as if spell-bound—fearful, perhaps, of severing an invisible thread that tied them together at that moment.

It had been severed, nonetheless.

Already aroused, these provocative thoughts made Gabriel's cock ached with need. But to touch himself, to find his own release, would be a sin of the heart, not just of the body. So, he fisted his hands into the straw and lay still, resolved to resist any and all temptation.

In the end, he wandered out to the well and doused his head with a bucket of water, gasping as he shook the drops from his hair. He then gasped again as the drips snaked chilly tracks down his spine and over his chest. But the shock of it cooled his cravings.

He glanced up at the sky, thankful to see stars rather than clouds. Hopefully, the day ahead would be less miserable than its predecessor and, God willing, he would be at Furness Abbey by nightfall.

Eager to be gone, he readied himself and set out beneath a dark, pre-dawn sky. Kadar, at least, seemed rested, judging by the bounce in his step. The miles soon disappeared beneath his hooves.

As dawn arrived, spilling its golden light across the

valleys and hills, Gabriel felt his spirit stir with something akin to optimism. He welcomed the sensation. The road ahead—metaphorical as well as literal—seemed brighter.

They made good time. Or rather, Kadar did, the horse showing little sign of fatigue as he'd continued to dispatch the miles. Gabriel, as a Templar, had attracted attention from others on the road—some of it benign, some of it dubious, but none of it threatening. Now, late in the afternoon, with only a few miles remaining, he halted Kadar by a marshland stream and dismounted. The horse nickered with pleasure and lowered his head to drink.

Gabriel rolled his shoulders, pushed the stiffness from his spine, and emptied his bladder into a solitary patch of bracken. As he waited for Kadar to drink his fill, a vague feeling of apprehension crept into his gut. He glanced about, seeing no sign of life other than the tough little mountain sheep, common to the region, grazing on wiry grass.

It was a desolate spot. Little more than moorland, in truth. Stalks of cotton-grass bobbed their white feathered heads in the breeze, and patches of heather clambered over the hillsides. The occasional copse of stunted trees, limbs bent and twisted by the persistent wind, might offer a traveller some semblance of shelter, but the land was otherwise bare.

A cloud passed over the sun, its sudden shadow drawing Gabriel's gaze skyward. Broken patches of cloud drifted aloft, none of them promising rain. Yet the feeling of unease remained. And he'd long since learned to trust it. As if in affirmation, Kadar lifted his dripping muzzle from the stream, pricked his ears, and stamped a back hoof.

Gabriel settled his hand on his sword hilt. Senses honed, he shifted his gaze to the road, a section of which lay within clear sight, the rest obscured as it snaked off into the knolls and hollows of the landscape. He cocked his head, catching the sound of hooves on the wind. Horsemen, coming toward him from the north. Several of them, it seemed.

A low rumble came from Kadar's chest as the group came into view. Four men, armed, their horses spurred into an easy canter. No identifying banners that Gabriel could see. The hair on his nape bristled like hackles. Kadar snorted and showed his teeth.

They almost rode past but noticed Gabriel at the last moment and shared a triumphant smirk as they pulled their horses to a halt. Gabriel prayed his instinct was wrong—instinct that told him the men had been looking for him. They turned and rode back, forming a half-circle on the road, blocking his way. It was a calculated move, Gabriel knew. One intended to intimidate.

His instinct had been correct. He recognized the men as those he'd seen at the hostelry the previous night. Their dark scrutiny brought to mind a wolf pack, eyeing their prey. One of the men pasted a false smile on his face and shifted in the saddle. "Good eve, Templar. We meet again, it seems."

"Good eve to you too." Gabriel held the man's gaze. "And I trust it will stay that way."

The smiled vanished. "You sneaked away before dawn this morning. What are you about?"

Gabriel shrugged. "What concern is it of yours?"

A perceptible ripple of disapproval passed through the group.

"'Tis a concern with merit," the man replied. "Your lot are being arrested here in England, yet I understand the Bruce has granted you sanctuary in his ill-gotten lands to the north, and I must ask myself why he would do that." A cold smirk curved his mouth. "That holy garb no longer protects you here, Templar. Answer the question."

"And, in case you haven't noticed," another man piped up, "we are four to your one."

"I can count." Gabriel stroked his thumb over the cross carved into the pommel of his sword. "I warrant not one of you would be challenging me on your own."

Eyes narrowing, the same man half-drew his sword. "Watch your tongue."

"Holy, my arse," another said, and spat on the ground. "They're burning them by the dozen in France. 'Tis said they worship the Devil and suck each other's cocks. Is that true?"

Gabriel's gut tightened in anger. "None of the accusations against us are true."

The man who had first spoken gave a scornful laugh. "We're waiting, Templar. Explain your presence here, or pay the price."

No matter his response, Gabriel knew a price would be exacted. Hostility leached from these men like a rotten stench. They didn't want answers. They only wanted blood. This sparring with words was merely a precursor to the inevitable. He cast a quick glance to the north, wondering if, at that precise moment, he occupied the thoughts of a young woman who had found a place in his heart. He hoped so. It seemed important, somehow.

Will I ever see you again?

God willing.

Gabriel regarded the men and assessed his situation. *Dire* came to mind. They had him cornered. Outnumbered. It would be prudent, then, to capitulate to their dominance. To yield without resistance, turn the other cheek, and beg for mercy.

But Gabriel was a Knight of the Temple.

So, he crossed himself, uttered a prayer, and drew his sword.

Chapter Thirteen

Castle Cathan
Western Highlands of Scotland
Monday, the 12ᵗʰ day of June, year of the Lord, 1308

Standing atop the battlements, Ewan pushed his cloak back from his shoulders and looked to the south. Not that he could see anything. Fog had rolled in during the night, blanketing land and sea. The muffled sound of the waves carried to where he stood, as did the endless cries of seabirds. He paid them little mind.

Maybe today, he thought. Maybe today they would have news. A missive that would put his heart and mind to rest.

Eight months had passed since Ewan had fled to Scotland with Gabriel and Jacques. Nigh on five weeks had passed since, against Ewan's better judgement, Gabriel had set out for England. They should have had news by now, but there had been no word. Nothing.

Ewan reflected how Gabriel, on a daily basis, did three things without fail. He prayed, he practiced with his sword, and he wrote. Something must have gone wrong. Ewan felt certain of it.

"Where are you, Brother?" he muttered, squinting into the fog. "Why have we not heard from you?"

"Ah, here you are." Duncan emerged from the fog and came to stand beside him. "I cannae find my hand in front of my face in this shite. You're needed inside, Ewan."

The sober tone of the clan steward made Ewan frown. He shifted his gaze toward the keep, which lay hidden behind a veil of fog.

"Why?" he asked, already moving toward the stairs. "Is something wrong? Is Cristie all right?"

So far, his young wife had carried the babe with little trouble, but Ewan, whose own mother had died shortly after his birth, knew well the risks of child-bearing.

"Your lady is quite well." The man cleared his throat. "But a missive has arrived. Jacques is waiting for you in the great hall."

"A missive? When did that get here?" Ewan hurried down the steps and strode across the courtyard. "Is it from Gabriel?"

"It came while you were in the chapel," Duncan replied. "'Twas simply addressed to the Templars in residence."

"Then it must be from Gabriel," Ewan muttered, praying he was wrong about the sudden feeling of dread in the pit of his stomach.

"God help us, 'tis what I feared. He should have never have left." Hand shaking as he held the parchment, Ewan read the abbot's neatly scribed words over again, unwilling to accept the tragedy they described. "Gravely wounded, though it doesnae say how, exactly."

"I must go to him," Jacques said. "I'll leave at dawn."

"I pray to God he yet lives." Ewan read the missive for the third time, as if doing so might change its tragic contents. "This was written nine days ago."

"Must you go, Jacques?" Morag asked, hands clasped, prayer-like, at her chest, "'Tis no' safe down there. What if you're set upon as well?"

"Well, it won't be by the men who attacked Gabriel," Jacques replied, his expression grim, "since he dispatched three of them and wounded the fourth."

"Aye, but..." Morag shook her head. "I'm sure there are plenty more just like them."

Jacques gave her a sober smile. "I have to go, Morag. He's our brother."

Ewan settled an arm around Cristie's shoulders. "I'd go myself if I didnae have a wee wife with a child on the way."

Cristie gave him an incredulous look. "'Twould not be wise, *mo ghràidh*. They attacked a Sasunnach in his own country. Imagine what they'd do to a Scot."

"If not for precisely that reason, I'd send Brody with you, Jacques," Ruaidri said, "but I cannae put the man's life at risk." He stood by the open window, his back to them. A breeze had stirred with the rising of the sun, clearing much of the fog. But it did little to clear the gloom in his private chamber. He turned to face them, his gaze coming to rest on Jacques. "And I echo Ewan's prayer that Gabriel still lives, and this undertaking of yours willnae be for naught."

"He lives," Jacques replied. "I refuse to believe otherwise. As for sending someone with me, it won't be necessary. I'll remove all the insignia before I cross the border. No one will know I'm a Templar."

Ruaidri raised a brow. "Isn't that against your code?"

Jacques shrugged. "To quote Hippocrates, desperate times call for desperate measures. Gabriel should have done the same. By displaying his allegiance to the order, he took the risk of being set upon by those who believe the accusations against us. We are no longer viewed as we once were."

"Sadly true," Ewan said, "though I suspect our brother would see such an action as a silent admission of guilt."

"Martyrdom can be as foolish as it is noble," Jacques replied. "Gabriel's death would serve no purpose."

Ruaidri left his spot by the window. "Let me see that missive, Ewan. There's something about it that bothers me. Something that doesnae add up."

Ewan handed it over. "What?"

Frowning, Ruaidri cast his eyes over the parchment. "It says here that Gabriel was attacked on his way to the abbey."

"Aye, so?"

"So, we've all be wondering why he hasnae written. He left here, what, five weeks ago? Barring incident, it shouldnae have taken more than a sennight—ten days, maybe—to reach the abbey. Going by the date on this missive, it took him almost a month to get there." He handed the parchment back. "Why? Where has he been the rest of the time?"

"Good question," Ewan murmured, re-reading the abbot's words. "Something obviously took him away from his journey."

"I guess I'll find out what when I get there." Jacques stood. "If you'll excuse me, *mes amis*, I must make preparations."

Morag rose too. "I'll go and arrange some food for you," she mumbled, and followed Jacques from the room.

Ewan gave Ruaidri a telling glance. "If anything happens to Jacques, she'll be heartbroken."

"Aye." Ruaidri heaved a sigh. "But I reckon she'll be heartbroken anyway, at some point."

Chapter Fourteen

Breanna sat on the church steps twirling a dandelion-clock between her fingers. "It's been fifteen days, Father," she said, making a silent wish as she blew on the soft, downy seeds. They floated off, like tiny fairies, to snatch a ride on the evening breeze. Breanna wondered, vaguely, how far the scatterings might go and where they would land. "Fifteen days and not a word. I should have heard from him by now. I have an awful feeling something has happened to him."

She'd had the feeling for a while—a vague sense of unease that stayed with her day and night. She refused to believe he'd forgotten about her. He'd promised he'd send word, and Gabriel would never break a promise. Of that, she was certain.

Father Dunstan parted with a grunt as he settled himself beside her. "Curse these old bones," he said, rubbing a knee. "Don't fret, child. I doubt anything bad has happened to him. In all my years, I've never seen a man better able to defend himself. He's probably been occupied with other things." He cleared his throat. "Like preparing to take his final vows, for instance."

Breanna sighed at the priest's undertone. "I asked him to let me know when he'd arrived at the abbey, that's all." She blew the remaining seeds from the dandelion head and cast the stalk aside. "Surely, his vows will allow him to do that."

"And would you have replied to him if he'd

written?'

"Nay." She shrugged, her cheeks warming "Well, probably not."

Father Dunstan chuckled. "Let me assume that to mean 'yes', and in that case, if he hadn't replied a second time, I'd be hearing this same complaint from you." He grimaced and scratched his head. "Gabriel is a monk, Breanna. He's taken vows of celibacy and, despite what you might think, being celibate is not just about carnal restraint. It goes way beyond that. It demands a person's affection and love for God in its entirety. Gabriel's heart belongs to God. It can *only* belong to God. Any amorous feelings he might have had for you were sinful, and I must assume he has absolved himself of them. Any feelings you have for him must also be discarded, for they can serve no purpose."

"My feelings are those of simple concern, naught else," Breanna replied, recalling, for the thousandth time, the moment Gabriel had turned to look at her before he left. It had come and gone in a heartbeat, the impression that he was going to turn Kadar around and ride back to her. But then her uncle had said something. Something that had made Gabriel stay his course.

Even so, in her heart, she knew that he cared.

And, may God forgive her for lying to Father Dunstan. Her feelings for Gabriel were a good deal more than simple concern. Nor could they easily be discarded like some timeworn piece of clothing.

But of all those at Ghyllhead, the old priest was the

only one Breanna felt she could speak to about Gabriel. Doing so helped ease some of the weight from her mind, though Father Dunstan's priestly responses were never quite what she wanted to hear. Yet the logic of his reasoning, while poisonous to her hopes and dreams, could not be denied. Gabriel had always been clear about where his future lay. And it was not with her. It would never be with her. In truth, she would likely never see him again.

Maybe, after all, that was the sole cause of her uneasiness. *The agony of truth.*

"Gabriel is quite well, I'm sure." Father Dunstan grunted again as he rose to his feet. "Thank you for the bread and flowers, my dear. If you'll excuse me, I have to sound Vespers. I suggest you send that lazy fellow back to the woods and get yourself back to Ghyllhead before your uncle comes looking for you. I'll send Alfred out. He's likely fallen asleep."

Breanna muttered a farewell to the priest and glanced down at Theo, who lay curled up beside her on the step. The fox met her gaze without lifting his head, and acknowledged it with a twitch of his tail. He'd been subdued since Gabriel's departure. Markedly so.

She scratched behind his ear. "I miss him too, Theo," she whispered, the confession bringing tears to her eyes. "I miss him very much."

Theo's ribcage rose and fell, and his tail twitched once more.

Walter met them at the gates, dismissing Alfred

before he spoke to Breanna.

"Your uncle is looking for you, my lady," he said. "He's in the solar and asked that you go there immediately upon your return."

"He knew I was going to St Bega's," she said, feeling a need to defend her absence. "I asked his permission, and he gave it."

"Aye, I know." Walter smiled. "I don't think you're in any trouble. A missive came while you were gone. I suspect it might have something to do with that."

A missive? Heart racing, Breanna thanked Walter and hurried away. Perhaps Gabriel had written at last. That he'd sent word to her uncle and not her irked a little, but it made sense. It was, after all, more appropriate, given his situation.

She slowed her hasty step as she approached the solar, took a calming breath, and smoothed her skirts. Then, with chin raised and a smile on her face, she entered.

Goblet in hand, Savaric sat by the empty fireplace saying something to Linette, who was perched on a stool at his feet.

"Ah, good, here she is," he said, rising to his feet as Breanna entered.

"Walter said you wanted to see me, Uncle."

"Indeed." Smiling, he set his goblet down and gestured to an empty chair opposite his own. "Close the door behind you and then sit, please."

She did as bid, a niggle of apprehension rising in her belly. Savaric's smile stretched from one ear to the next. He appeared to be ecstatic, for want of a better word. Why would word of Gabriel's arrival prompt such a response?

"I have two announcements to make," he said, extending a hand to Linette, who took it and rose to his side. "One concerns your aunt, the other concerns you. For now, you'll repeat nothing of what you hear till after this evening's meal, when I shall make the news official. Understood?"

Breanna's apprehension grew. "What news, Uncle?"

Still smiling, Savaric looped an arm around his wife's waist. "Linette is with child," he said, gazing at his wife with blatant fondness. "She is carrying my heir."

Breanna gasped and shot to her feet. "Oh, but that is *wonderful* news." She approached and kissed Linette on the cheek. "I'm so happy for you, my lady. Do you know when the child is due?"

"I felt the babe quicken last night." Linette's hand fell to her abdomen. "So, Winifred thinks it will arrive late in the autumn."

"A cousin for me," Breanna said, clapping her hands. "How exciting. I cannot wait to meet him or her."

There followed a moment of silence. Savaric's smile wavered a little as he released Linette and picked up a scroll from a nearby table.

"The second announcement concerns you, Breanna. I trust you'll be as equally happy when you hear it."

The apprehension returned. "What is it?"

He raised the scroll and cleared his throat. "I have

secured a contract of marriage for you with Baron Mathias Talbot's second son. His name is—"

"Nay!" Breanna shook her head. "Nay, Uncle, forgive me, but I have no desire to marry anyone."

Linette huffed. "'Tis not for you to decide, Breanna. The agreement has already been made."

Scowling, Breanna hugged herself. "An agreement I knew nothing about till this moment."

Savaric narrowed his eyes. "I shall finish what I was saying. His name is Ansell. He is a knight, and his father holds Brierfield, which is a good-sized barony in Northumberland. The wedding has been set for the end of August and will take place at Brierfield. Given your status, this is a good match for you."

"Given my status?"

He heaved a sigh. "You're my ward, Breanna, not my heir. Without me to provide a dowry, you would have nothing of significance to bring to the marriage table."

"Oh, of course. A business agreement." Breanna gave a bitter laugh. "So, how much am I worth?"

She knew, as soon as she finished speaking, that she'd gone too far. Linette's gasp and the change in her uncle's demeanor was instant. Jaw clenched, he approached to within an arm's length and glared down at her.

"I have never had you whipped, though God only knows you've deserved it enough times over the years," he said, through gritted teeth. "You will respect who I am, what I have done for you, and you will apologize for that remark immediately, or I swear

I'll take a switch to your hide myself."

Seeing the pain in her uncle's eyes brought tears to her own. "I'm sorry, Uncle. I regret what I said, truly. It's just that I… I didn't expect this. 'Tis a shock."

Savaric looked away for a moment. "Christ give me strength," he muttered, his expression wretched as he turned back. "You remind me so much of my sister. She was as you are, defiant and impulsive, and she paid the price for it, by God. I do not want the same for you, and neither, I suspect, would she."

Breanna knew she had no valid argument. What could she say, after all? That she didn't want to marry Ansell because she loved another man? A Templar, no less, who had already made his choice? *What choice do I have?*

"A convent," Linette said. "If she continues to defy you, Husband, send her to a convent."

Savaric grunted. "Is that what you want, Breanna? Would you prefer a cloistered life over marriage?"

Would I? The answer came quickly, bringing a shudder with it. "Nay."

"Then I'll have no more defiance." He ran a hand through his hair. "I realized you might be…disquieted by this, so in an effort to make things easier, I've arranged for Ansell to visit Ghyllhead at the end of the month. You'll at least, then, have a chance to meet your future husband before the wedding and get to know him a little."

Breanna tried to muster some enthusiasm but failed. "Thank you, Uncle."

"That's all?" His brows lifted. "I expected

questions, at least."

"About what?"

"Your betrothed." He shrugged. "Ask, if you have them. Your curiosity, I will tolerate."

Until that moment, it had never occurred to Breanna how little control she had over her own life. No control at all, in truth. The realization sliced through her hopes and dreams like a blade, striking a lethal blow.

"My curiosity serves no purpose, Uncle. Knowing the man's age, whether he is fat or thin, or thinks naught of beating a woman, will change nothing. The decision about my future has already been made." She lifted her chin. "May I go now?"

A fleeting expression of sadness crossed Savaric's face. "Aye, you may go, Breanna, but you will not speak of this to anyone until after the announcement has been made."

Chapter Fifteen

Jacques halted his horse at the crest of the hill and gazed down into the wooded vale, his nine-day journey almost at an end. The sandstone walls of Furness Abbey, brushed by the soft evening light, glowed like the dying embers of a fire. Under any other circumstances, he would have considered it to be an astounding sight.

But until he'd learned the truth of Gabriel's fate, he could not rejoice in the spectacle. His stomach twisted with trepidation as he dismounted and led his horse onward.

"My name is Jacques Aznar, and I'm a knight of the Temple," he said, handing the abbot's letter to a rather robust lay-monk who'd greeted him at the gate. "I'm here in response to that missive. I'm here to see Brother Gabriel Fitzalan."

Please tell me he still lives.

The monk barely glanced at the missive. His smile vanished, replaced by an expression of sympathy that one might bestow upon a bereaved family member. Jacques held his breath.

"Please, come with me," the monk said. "I'm certain the abbot will see you right away."

Jacques had no choice but to ask. "Does my brother still live?"

The monk gave him a startled glance. "Oh, yes, friend. He still lives. I beg your pardon. I should have made that clear."

An invisible weight tumbled from Jacques'

shoulders. Until that moment, he hadn't realized how heavy it had been. "Thank God," he murmured.

The monk's jowls wobbled as he nodded his agreement. "You may tether your horse there." He gestured to a rail outside one of the abbey buildings. "I'll make sure it's tended. This is the guest house. Please wait in the vestibule while I locate Father Simon. It shouldn't take long. There's fruit and water on the table. Help yourself."

Jacques paced as he waited. Though beyond relieved that Gabriel was still alive, the monk's reaction still bothered him. 'Gravely wounded', the abbot's letter had said. He had yet to find out what that meant.

After a short time, the door opened and a man entered, his expression at first taut, but softening at the sight of Jacques. Without pause, he approached, reached for Jacques' hand, and placed it between both of his own, his grip confident and warm. Tall and lean, the man was younger than Jacques had envisioned—not much older than himself, it seemed. The hair on his tonsured head glinted with gold, and the smile he gave was unforced and genuine.

"Welcome to Furness Abbey," the man said, his eyes alight with interest. "I only regret that your visit is not due to better circumstances. I'm Father Simon, the abbot of this cloister. And you, my son, are a prayer answered." A measure of puzzlement showed on his face as studied Jacques' attire. "I understand you are also a knight of the Temple."

"I am indeed, Father." Jacques glanced down at his

black tunic. "Though 'tis better not to proclaim it these days."

"As Gabriel sadly discovered." The abbot's expression sobered once more. "How long can you stay?"

"As long as I'm needed. I have no agenda."

"Good. And I've no doubt you're eager to see him." The abbot opened the door and gestured outside. "But I think it best I speak with you first, and somewhere a little more agreeable."

Jacques did not miss the hint of foreboding in the abbot's words. "Has he been maimed, Father?"

"Nay, though he is still far from physically sound. He sleeps a lot, and we let him. Time and rest are the best medicines for now." They stepped out and headed down the path toward the great church. "To begin," the abbot continued, "the attack took place about an hour's ride from here. Four men, as you know, set upon him. He killed three during the fight, and the fourth has since died of his injuries."

A chill touched the nape of Jacques neck. "He must have fought like a madman."

"Indeed, but he did not emerge unscathed. He took a blade to the abdomen. From a dagger, undoubtedly, judging by the size of the wound. When the fight ended, Gabriel hoisted the injured man onto one of the other horses, got back on his own horse, and continued on to the abbey with the injured man in tow." The abbot assumed a smile and muttered a greeting to a couple of passing monks. Then his smile vanished again. "When he arrived at the abbey gates we thought, at first glance, that his horse had been wounded, since it was covered in blood on its left side. We quickly realized it was not the horse's blood at all."

Jacques tasted bile. "Gabriel's."

Expression grim, the abbot nodded. "He collapsed moments after he passed through the gates. In truth, 'tis a miracle he made it to the abbey at all. I gave him the last rites then and there. I truly did not believe he'd survive the night."

Jacques crossed himself. "Thank God he did."

"Not without a struggle. He was weaker than an infant. His battle for survival continued for days afterwards and is still, frankly, ongoing. How long have you known Gabriel, my son?"

"Ever since he returned from the Levant, so... four years."

"And how well do you know him?"

Jacques frowned at the question. "Well enough, I think, Father. Gabriel is a valued friend and brother, and I would not hesitate to trust him with my life. He's everything a Templar knight should be."

"A worthy accolade, indeed," the abbot replied.

The path led into the abbey cloisters—a sheltered walkway overlooking a courtyard garden. Long shadows of evening crisscrossed the herb and flowerbeds, while swallows swooped here and there, snatching their last meal of the day from the air. Jacques inhaled the sweet scents of lavender and thyme. "A peaceful place," he said, as much to himself as to the abbot.

"Yes, it is. We are very blessed." The abbot halted by a stone bench and sat down, indicating with a wave of his hand that Jacques should do likewise. "I know, from what Gabriel has said, that he values your friendship also. But what of his past? Has he ever spoken of it to you?"

Jacques settled himself as directed. "Not in any great detail. I know his mother died when he was a child, and that his father was a minor noble who, I believe, died in battle. He has no siblings. At least, he's never mentioned the existence of any."

The abbot grunted. "He's an only child. And yes, his father died in a Welsh skirmish a few weeks before Gabriel acquired his spurs. Father and son were not close, however. Ralf Fitzalan was, by all accounts, a violent man. As for Gabriel's mother..." The abbot fingered the paternoster at his belt. "She supposedly died in childbirth soon after Gabriel was sent out to foster."

"Supposedly?"

"There is some doubt as to the cause of her demise."

"Hmm. I've never heard Gabriel speak of it." Jacques fidgeted. *Why is all this necessary?*

"I have my reasons for telling you this," the abbot said, as if reading Jacques' thoughts. "I know you're eager to see him, but please bear with me a little longer."

Jacques gave a resigned smile. "Forgive me, Father," he said. "My Basque blood lacks patience."

The abbot gave a brief smile and continued.

"Unlike many young fosters, Gabriel was actually a literate child. His mother taught him to read and write at a young age."

Jacques gave a nod. "The man writes almost as much as he prays. He had to leave most of his work behind when we fled France. I never heard him complain, but I'm certain it was hard on him."

"Yet he has not written a word since he came here."

"He's too weak to do so?"

"He was. Now, though, he shows no interest in it. But I digress." The abbot fingered his paternoster again. "I happen to know he wrote letters to his mother while he was being fostered."

Jacques frowned at the undertone in the abbot's voice. "Not so unusual he should do so."

"I agree. Oddly, however, he never had a response. It wasn't until a year later that he found out she'd died a short time after he left."

"His father never told him?"

"Nay," came the reply. "Nor does Gabriel believe the story of her death."

"What does he believe?"

"That she died at the hands of his father who, as I said, was a violent man."

Jacques' eyes widened. "He told you this?"

"When he first heard the news, aye." The abbot cleared his throat. "Gabriel fostered with Lord John Egerton of Leicester. John was my father, may God rest his soul. I'm John's second son. I've known Gabriel since he was seven years old. He was only eight when he received news of his mother's death. I had just entered my thirteenth year, and, to this day, I can clearly remember his reaction. Gabriel blamed himself for not being there to protect her. I swear I have never, before or since, seen a child so filled with rage."

"I know nothing of this." Jacques ran a hand through his hair. "'Tis true Gabriel has always been a quiet one. Solemn to the point of sombre. But why are you telling me this now? Is it relevant?"

"It might be." The abbot rose. "Something is eating at Gabriel's soul, my son, and I've been unable to discover what it is. I'm hoping and praying you might succeed where I have failed, since I believe doing so is crucial to his healing. Knowing something of his past might help you to understand his mental plight."

"He was conflicted when he left Scotland," Jacques said. "'Tis why he left. He said he hoped to find his path. The persecution of our order has hit him very hard."

"I know, but I believe there's more to it than that. There's something he's not telling us."

"Did he say where he was before he came to Furness? Perhaps something happened there."

Frowning, the abbot paused his stride again. "Before he came to Furness? I don't understand."

Jacques grimaced. "Gabriel left Scotland six weeks ago, Father. We heard nothing of him till we received your missive."

"Six…?" An expression of shock flew across the abbot's face. "Then where, under God's great sky, has he been?"

"A good question." Jacques rubbed the back of his neck. "And more importantly, why would he not speak of it?"

"I cannot begin to know," the abbot replied, "though I suspect it must play a part, since he has chosen not to share it. I pray he will share it with you. I thank God you're here, my son."

Chapter Sixteen

The bell pealed out a summons to vespers. Gabriel gripped the arms of his chair, tempted to call for help. He felt a little stronger today. Maybe then, with assistance, he might manage the walk to the church and join the monks for the evening service.

He hoisted himself to his feet, legs trembling as they held his weight. So far, so good. He took one step and then another, eyeing the doorway as if it were a mile away.

It might as well have been.

"God help me," he muttered, and took another faltering step just as the soft rap of a knuckle fell upon his door.

"Perfect timing," Gabriel said. "Please come in."

The door yawned open to reveal Jacques standing on the threshold. Gabriel's eyes blurred with tears at the sight. Such were his dreams these days, creating joyous possibilities from the impossible, and falsely granting prayers that God, so far, had not heard. For his friend could not actually be there. Could he?

"Greetings, Brother," Jacques said, over the continued clang of the church bell. "It does my heart good to see you."

Gabriel clenched and unclenched his fists as he began to doubt the validity of this dream. He feared, instead, that it might be an illusion, conjured up by a mind that had finally sailed past the point of sanity. He held out a hand of welcome to see what would happen. An illusion, after all, would not be solid.

Would not be warm.

"Please, God," he whispered, reaching. "Please."

Jacques' hand tightened around his, as solid and as warm as mortal flesh could be. That same, strong hand then pulled him into an embrace, holding him close. Supporting him.

"It's all right, my friend," Jacques said. "I have you."

A groan escaped from Gabriel's throat, wrenched free by an indescribable sense of solace. His breath shuddered from his lungs as his legs gave way. Not that it mattered. He knew his brother would never let him fall.

"Perfect timing," he said and slid into darkness.

She had the face of an angel.

Gabriel knew that to be so, for he'd seen her likeness, carved in stone, gazing down at him in church. She only lacked the wings. He watched her now, her head bent over her work, lips moving in silent prayer. She prayed all the time, although he rarely heard the words spoken. Gabriel supposed it didn't really matter as long as God could hear them. And she'd once told him God heard everything. Every prayer. Every thought. Since then, Gabriel had tried to keep his words and his thoughts kindly, and made sure to pardon himself for any transgressions.

Voices, their words muffled, drifted through the thick, wooden door from the hallway beyond, and her lips stopped moving. So did her needle. She kept her head bowed, staring at the piece of embroidery in her lap. Gabriel wondered why her hands were trembling.

Then something fell from her eye. A tiny jewel. A brief spark of light.

A tear.

"He is returned." She lifted her gaze to his and, all at once Gabriel understood why her hands trembled. "You must go now, mon petit."

The door opened, and a man wearing Satan's face stepped into the room. Gabriel knew that to be so, for Father Bertrand had described the fallen angel to him in detail; flesh reddened by hatred, eyes wild and bulging, lips curled back like those of a rabid dog.

"You must always fight against evil, Gabriel," the priest had said. "It must never be allowed to prevail."

But he had not fought the last time. Or the time before that. Or any other time Satan had walked through that door. Instead, in the cold clutches of fear, he had run off to hide in his room.

"Go, mon petit," she repeated, her voice devoid of emotion. "Go now."

But he had never been able to hide from the sound of her screams. And he could not bear the thought of hearing them again.

"Nay, Maman." He rose to his feet, lifted his chin, and looked Satan in the eye. "Not this time."

Gabriel opened his eyes to candlelight. "Christ help me," he whispered, feeling the rapid thud of his heart in his throat.

"Calm yourself, Brother." A cool hand touched his

brow. "It was just a dream."

Gabriel groaned, reality returning as he took hold of Jacques' arm and sat up, blinking as his eyes adjusted. "Jacques. Forgive me. Did I wake you?"

"Nay. I wasn't asleep." Jacques turned away and poured water in to a cup. "Here, drink this."

The liquid soothed his dry throat. "My thanks." He handed the cup back and studied his friend, trying to feel a smidgen of guilt for being the cause of his journey from Scotland. But he felt only relief and gratitude. "I can scarce believe you're here. I thought my mind was playing tricks when you opened the door. How long can you stay?"

"'Till you tell me to leave," Jacques replied. "I'm here for as long as you need me, Brother."

Gabriel noticed the pallet on the floor, obviously put there for Jacques' use. "As you have undoubtedly surmised," he said, "things have not quite gone as planned. I assume Father Simon wrote to you."

"Aye." Jacques settled onto a chair beside Gabriel's bed. "And thank God he did. He also asked me to check your wound. Does it bother you still?"

"Not much." Gabriel placed his hand atop the injury. "It has healed well."

"Thank God you're still alive." Jacques' lip furled. "Unlike the whoresons who tried to kill you."

"They almost succeeded."

"Four men, Gabriel?" Jacques gave him an incredulous look. "Single handed?"

He gave a half shrug. "I suppose I wasn't ready to die."

"And you brought the injured man back here?" Jacques grimaced. "I doubt I'd have been so merciful."

"It would probably have been more merciful to finish him, since he died anyway, but he begged me for help." Gabriel fidgeted at the memory. "Enough of that. What news of Castle Cathan?"

Jacques' taut expression slackened. "Everyone there is praying for you, Brother."

"I appreciate that." He glanced at the window. "Do you have any idea of the hour?"

"A little before dawn, I should think."

"With your help, then, I'd like to take some air."

Jacques looked dubious. "I'm not sure that's wise. You need to rest."

"I am weary of resting." Gabriel swung his legs off the side of the bed and rose, unsteadily, to his feet. "I find these walls oppressive of late. Humour me, Brother."

"Very well." Jacques pulled the blanket from the bed and draped it around Gabriel's shoulders. "Here. Lean on me."

A short while later, exhausted but triumphant, Gabriel settled on a stone bench that nestled against the eastern wall of the great church. He rested at ease beside his friend, thankful for his presence. Enjoying the peace of the night, he felt no obligation to converse. Jacques knew him well enough, and knew he wasn't one for idle talk. A compulsion to speak arose within him all the same.

"I'm beyond grateful that you're here, Brother."

"I know it," Jacques replied. "I also know you would have done the same for me."

"Without question." With relish, Gabriel breathed in a lungful of cool air and tipped his head back to gaze at the bright, crescent moon hanging overhead. For the first time in many days, the burden on his spirit lessened. "Without question."

But what of the others in need of help? How many Templars will die alone this night, caged in French prisons, falsely accused, tortured and starved?

He closed his eyes, offered up a silent prayer for those in torment, and then steered his thoughts away from the oppressive images. But he knew the fabrications against the Order would continue, and probably long into the future.

Unbidden, an image of young Flip, with his grubby face and bloodied nose, came to mind. Even children, it seemed, harboured misconceptions about the Templars, although Gabriel couldn't help but smile as he recalled Flip's questions. No doubt the boy had misunderstood the concept of celibacy, but the question had been answered anyway.

Templars have mothers and sisters. Some even have wives. Women they love.

Gabriel had not been celibate all his adult life, but none of the women he'd taken to his bed had ever stirred more than his lust.

Breanna, untouched as she was, had stirred something within him that he still did not recognize. Like a demon, it possessed him with a ferocity that burned like fire. He had tried and failed to exorcise it.

Was it love? Or simply desire? Whatever it was, it would not let go.

"I'm sworn to celibacy, I cannot marry."

"You could renounce your vows if you wished."

"That will not happen."

"Will I ever see you again?"

"If God wills it."

A door opened in his mind, and light poured out like a waterfall, near blinding him with its brilliance. In its midst, the familiar silhouette of a woman. She moved toward him, reached out a hand, and called his name.

He answered, and she stepped out of the light and moved toward him, cheeks scarred by the trails of her tears.

"I hoped you might find a place for me in your heart as well," she said.

"You do have a place in my heart, Breanna. You will always have it."

Gabriel opened his eyes and the images in his head flew into oblivion like smoke in the wind. It took him a moment to remember where he was. To his bewilderment, the stars had faded, though a pale crescent moon still hung in the sky. A silver mist now drifted over the dew-laden grass, and birdsong rang out from the surrounding trees. Gabriel worked a kink from his neck and wondered why his heart felt so heavy.

"I slept?"

"For a while, aye." Jacques regarded him. "Are you

cold? Maybe we should go inside."

"Nay, I'm fine." He winced as he shifted. "They'll be sounding Lauds soon. I've yet to attend a church service here. I'd like to go."

"Don't overtax yourself, Brother. You're still weak."

"I'm fine," he repeated.

Jacques heaved a sigh and leaned forward, resting his elbows on his knees as he appeared to examine the ground at his feet. "Who's Breanna?"

Startled, Gabriel looked at him. "I spoke her name?"

"Several times." Jacques slanted a sideways glance at him. "Who is she?"

"She is..." Gabriel grimaced and scratched at the stubble on his chin. "She is someone I'm trying hard to forget."

"Then it would appear you are not succeeding." Jacques heaved a soft sigh. "What happened, Gabriel? Where were you before you came to the abbey? You seem to have lost a week or two."

Gabriel gazed off into the distance, half-expecting, or perhaps hoping, to see a fox emerge from the trees.

"Nay, those weeks are not lost," he replied. "I remember every detail. And I can't decide if that's a blessing or a curse."

Jacques straightened. "Tell me."

Gabriel failed to suppress a shiver. "'Tis a long story."

"Then you can tell it to me indoors." Jacques stood and offered a hand. "Come on, Gabriel. No more arguments. You're shivering."

The church bell rang, making him jump. "Lauds first," he said, hoisting himself up with Jacques' help. "Please, Brother. I want to go. I *need* to go."

Jacques looked at him for a moment. "Then we'll go," he said, his voice thick with emotion. "Whatever you need, Gabriel. Whatever you need."

"She made you *laugh*?"

"Often."

"I have to meet this woman." A smile pulled at Jacques' mouth. "I'm intrigued to learn how she found a way into your sanctimonious heart. Of course, rescuing her from the forest would have helped your cause. She undoubtedly sees you as a hero."

"I fail to understand your amusement, Jacques, nor do I begin to share it." Gabriel, stretched out on his narrow bed, rubbed at his temple. A headache had arisen during the church service and still lingered, banging like a drum. "I am trying to discard these… these feelings."

After attending Lauds, they'd returned to Gabriel's cell, where he'd proceeded to tell Jacques about his days spent at Ghyllhead, and specifically about Breanna. Doing so had deepened his melancholy and left him exhausted.

It appeared Jacques noticed. "I fear you've overdone it tonight, my friend." He poured water into a cup and helped Gabriel sit before handing it to him.

"Drink this."

"My thanks." Gabriel took a gulp. "And I never had a *cause,* either. I'll be glad when this infatuation subsides."

"Infatuation? Nay, 'tis more than that. Love, I suspect. And love, my brother, isn't built on desert sand. It doesn't subside so easily. In fact, the longer you're away from her, the stronger it will likely become."

"I do not lo…" He frowned and uttered a mild curse.

"See?" Jacques sat and folded his arms. "You can't even deny it."

Gabriel huffed. "Love. Infatuation. It makes no difference. There's naught I can do about it."

"Did you tell her how you felt?"

"I told her she tempted me."

Jacques scoffed. "I warrant she swooned at that."

"I've taken vows, Jacques. I saw little point in baring all that lay in my soul. But she knew—we both knew—there was something between us."

"Vows can be renounced, Gabriel. Love is not a sin."

"She is promised to another."

His smile disappeared. "You failed to mention that."

"Again, I saw little point in doing so." He scowled into his cup. "I do not relish the feelings I have for Breanna because I can't act on them, vows or no. They have no place in my life."

"A life that will be spent here?"

He hesitated. "Aye, I think so."

"You *think* so? You're still not certain?"

"Nay, I'm not. I was certain of my life as a Templar, but now…" Gabriel swirled the water in his cup. "'Tis as if I'm looking for something, but I'm not sure what it is."

"You need more than that to commit to monastic life, my friend."

"I know."

Jacques frowned and turned his gaze to the window. "I wonder…"

"What?"

"Well, since, as you said, things have not quite gone according to plan in England, might you consider coming back to Scotland?"

The question, Gabriel realized, was one he'd hoped to hear. He ignored his pride and gave a truthful answer. "I might consider it, aye."

"Good. Then do so." Jacques filled his lungs and turned back to him. "In the meantime, we'll work on getting you back to full strength. Or close to it. All right?"

"Push against me. Harder. Aye, that's it. Excellent. There's a marked improvement over last week." Jacques released Gabriel's fisted hand. "How does it feel?"

Gabriel flexed his fingers and bent his right arm, clenching the muscle. "Much better."

"And your left side?"

"A slight sensation of pain. Nay, tightness, more like."

Jacques gave a nod. "Tomorrow, you'll pick up your sword."

"We'll have to practice outside the gates."

"Of course." Jacques gave a satisfied grin. "I'm thinking you need another two or three weeks of work. After that, if you feel ready, we can head back to Scotland."

Gabriel sat on the bench and flexed his hand again. "Sounds good."

And it did. Maybe the longer distance would help speed the healing of the wounds no one could see. Time, so far, had done little in that regard.

"You never wrote that letter to her, did you?"

Gabriel bit back a smile as he shook his head. It was uncanny how easily Jacques picked up on his thoughts. "Nay."

"Are you going to?"

"Nay." He rolled a touch of stiffness from his shoulders. "There's no point. De Clifford has his report on what happened to me. I've no doubt the information will be passed on to Savaric."

"Summer's end, you said."

"Jacques—"

"Breanna's not married yet." Jacques sat down beside him. "Nor will she be if we leave by the end of this month."

"Why are you doing this?" Gabriel rubbed the back of his neck. "You should be discouraging me. Telling me these feelings I have are sinful, which they are. Instead, you're doing the opposite."

"Because I know you, Gabriel. You're not a man given to frivolous thought or action. You always think before you speak and before you act. The only time I see you show any real passion is when you're praising God or using your blade. Why do you think Ewan teases you all the time? 'Tis to see that halo you wear wobble a little." Jacques sat back and folded his arms. "You're as close to being a saint as they come."

Gabriel gasped. "That is blasphemy, Brother."

"I jest. The point is, knowing you as I do, I don't believe your feelings for this girl are frivolous or sinful. I don't think you believe it, either." Jacques shook his head. "You cannot simply let this go, my friend. If you do, you'll regret it always."

"How many times must I remind you? Breanna is promised to another."

"And I guarantee she's as unhappy about it as you are. Speak to this Savaric. He sounds reasonable, and if he loves his niece as much as you've implied, he may well agree to annul the original agreement."

"After what happened with his wife, he'd never let me through the castle gates. Nor would he let me take Breanna to Scotland."

Jacques patted Gabriel's shoulder. "Cease being so defeatist, Brother. 'Tis not like you in the least."

"I'm being realistic."

"Then humour me." Jacques sighed. "We'll be passing the place anyway. We may as well pay them a visit."

Gabriel shook his head. "I don't think so, Jacques."

"Tell you what. We'll wait till we're passing the place, and then decide. Fair enough?"

"Do you swear not to mention it again till that time?"

"I swear."

"Fair enough."

Chapter Seventeen

Ansell had nice eyes, Breanna thought. Moss green, edged with soft brown lashes, and they crinkled when he laughed. He laughed a lot, too—perhaps a little too much and a little too loudly. A head of rich, brown curls softened the angular lines of his face and jaw. His nose was rather large. Noble, Breanna decided. And though not notably tall, he had a warrior's solid physique and held himself well. He was younger than Gabriel, but not by much. All in all, he was pleasing to look upon.

He'd arrived at Ghyllhead that afternoon, seated atop a hefty grey stallion and accompanied by two men, one of whom was his younger brother, Arthur. In preparation for his arrival, Breanna had been prodded and primped by Linette until she barely recognized herself. Her hair had been brushed till it shone, woven into a dozen braids—which, in turn, had been threaded with gold and burgundy silk to match her robe— and arranged in an intricate fashion about her head.

Introductions complete, they had gathered in the Great Hall and enjoyed a sumptuous feast. Well, most folks had. Breanna's stomach would not tolerate more than a few mouthfuls.

She sat on Ansell's left, fingering a small, gold locket at her throat, a gift from this green-eyed man who was to be her husband. Shaped like a small flower, it was engraved with a cross which, in turn, had been set with a garnet—a perfect match for her dress. She loved it and told Ansell so.

And she liked him. Or, at least, she didn't dislike him.

He had no idea, of course, that she wanted someone else. That, every single night, she went to bed wishing, praying, and dreaming that Gabriel would realize he'd made a terrible mistake and return to claim her.

It was folly on her part. Ridiculous, even. He'd been gone a month already—though it seemed longer—with no word. If something had happened to him, she told herself, they would have heard by now. So, obviously, he'd simply put her out of his mind. She wondered if a day would ever come when she didn't think about him.

She wasn't the only one who missed him, either. For the first few weeks after Gabriel's departure, Flip asked her daily if she'd heard anything. He no longer did so. He just went about his daily tasks and then retired to his mouse hole in the hayloft. Even Cedric conceded that he missed Gabriel's training sessions, though he also admitted that they'd nearly killed him. As for Theo, he'd perked up. Still, Breanna had the impression the bounce in the fox's step wasn't quite as before.

She'd stopped mentioning Gabriel to Father Dunstan, even during confession. The priest had told her to simply set her feelings aside, and that was that. As if she could.

"Are you still with us, my lady?"

Breanna blinked, lifted her chin from it had been

propped on her hand, and looked at Ansell. "My pardon, sir," she said, straightening. "I was wool-gathering."

"It has been a day with much excitement." He lifted her hand to his lips and let his mouth linger a moment. "I am beyond pleased with my future bride and look forward to getting to know her better. But if she is tired, she should perhaps get some rest. We can talk more on the morrow."

"Mmm, I am a little tired." Not exactly a lie. The truth was, she simply didn't feel any kind of connection to this man. Maybe it just needed time and effort. With Gabriel, it had been instant, and it was impossible not to compare. She prised her hand free. "If you'll excuse me, then, I'll see you in the morning."

"You will, my lady."

Breanna excused herself to her uncle.

"Well?" He glanced at Ansell. "Are you happy, child?"

She told him what he so obviously needed to hear. "Very, Uncle."

Linette followed her from the hall. As they got to the door, a loud guffaw of Ansell's laughter made Breanna turn and look. He'd obviously shared some joke with her uncle.

"So?" Linette looped her arm through Breanna's. "What do you think?"

"He seems pleasant enough," Breanna replied.

"He's handsome, is he not?"

"Yes, my lady, he is."

Yet, despite her declaration, she felt Linette's dubious scrutiny.

"You still have a fondness for that Templar, don't you?"

Breanna shrugged. "Does it matter? He's long gone."

Linette sighed. "I happen to know you spoke to him the morning he left. Did he tell you what prompted his early departure?"

"Nay, he wouldn't say." Breanna looked at her. "But I think he had a quarrel with my uncle."

"You are correct. And, as a result, Savaric told him to leave."

Breanna paused outside her chamber door. "What was it about?"

Linette waved a hand. "I doubt you'd want to know."

"Aye, I do." *Why mention it if you don't mean to tell me?* "What was it about?"

Linette parted with a sigh. "I'm afraid you'll not like what I'm about to say."

A cold finger touched the back of Breanna's neck. "I would have you say it anyway, my lady."

"Very well. The argument was about me."

"You?" Breanna frowned. "I don't understand."

"The day before, I'd gone looking for you. I was concerned about you, Breanna. You'd been depressed since the attack, and I thought to cheer you somehow. I looked everywhere, including the scriptorium. You were not there, but he was."

"Gabriel." Breanna nodded. "Yes, he told me he

was going to write his letter. I'd gone out to the stables to see Flip."

"Ah, well." She smiled. "That explains why I could not find you. Indeed, the Templar said he'd not seen you either, so I excused myself and turned to leave, but he called me back and we began to talk. I admit I made no effort to discourage him. Why would I? I did not believe him to be a threat. But then the conversation took a turn I did not like. He commented on my looks. Told me I was one of the most beautiful women he'd ever seen and that he found me tempting. Then he tried to force himself on me."

Breanna stared at Linette for a moment as the image of what she'd said played out in her mind. "I don't believe you," she said. "Gabriel would never do such a thing."

Linette gave a sardonic laugh. "Are you calling me a liar?" She practically shoved the inside of her wrist into Breanna's face. "He *marked* me here. Put bruises on me with the strength of his grip. Ask Savaric if you don't believe me. Your Templar was not as virtuous as he made himself out to be."

Breanna gasped. "Why are you doing this, my lady? I know you've always been jealous of me, but I've never understood why. You're far more beautiful than I, 'tis obvious my uncle loves you very much, and I cannot tell you how greatly it pleases me to see him so happy, especially now you're carrying his child. So why the malice? Why must you insist on spreading these lies? It serves no purpose that I can see."

"I'm telling you the truth," Linette replied, through gritted teeth. "The Templar put his hands on me."

Breanna gave her a scornful look. "If you swore this on the bible in front of the Pope himself, I would still not believe you," she said. "Gabriel would never force himself on you or any other woman."

"Then ask your uncle," Linette said, a flush on her cheeks. "Maybe 'tis you who are the jealous one, Breanna. You cannot accept that the Templar found me more appealing than you."

Rather than anger, Breanna felt a mix of pity and shame as she watched her aunt hurry away. Perhaps she should have been more sympathetic. After all, the woman was in a delicate condition. Then again, the tale she'd told had obviously been a fabrication, or a twisted version of the truth. She couldn't help wonder, though, what her uncle *had* said to Gabriel the day he'd left.

Craving solitude, Breanna attended to her own ablutions, closed the shutter, and slid between her sheets. Here, she gave little thought to Ansell or weddings or Linette's jealousies. They were considerations for the daylight hours and would be dealt with in the morning.

Here, in the silent privacy of her room and by the light of a single candle, Breanna spent time with Gabriel. She felt the security of his arms around her, listened to the soft tone of his voice, and saw a light in his eyes that shone solely for her.

A promise of love, unfulfilled.

Alone with her fantasies, she at last drifted into

sleep.

Chapter Eighteen

Breanna awoke to sound of baying hounds. Her uncle hadn't mentioned anything about a hunt being on the agenda, but it seemed one had now been arranged. She scrambled out of bed, opened her shutter, and peered out into a damp summer's morning.

Ghyllhead's hunting dogs were pawing at the castle gates as if trying to tear it down. Meanwhile, her uncle stood beside his horse talking to Cedric. He was wearing his sword, she noticed, a testament to an injury now little more than a scar. Ansell was already in the saddle, tussling with his excited stallion. The other riders, too, were mounted and waiting. Breanna watched as her uncle walked over to Arthur, Ansell's brother, and spoke to him. She couldn't hear what was being said but, from the way Arthur gestured, she had the distinct impression the words they shared were strong ones.

After a few moments, her uncle returned to his horse, and said something to Cedric before he mounted up, and gave the signal to open the gates. Dogs, horses, and men poured out, and the gates closed behind them.

Breanna cast an anxious glance toward the village and the church. Not that Theo would be there, necessarily—he could be anywhere, in truth—but she always associated him with that direction. There was always a risk the fox would run afoul of a hunt—that's how he'd come to be orphaned in the first place—but she sent up a little prayer for his safety anyway.

"Stay low, Theo," she whispered. "Please stay low."

A little later, she found Walter in the Great Hall nursing a cup of something and wearing a thoughtful expression.

"Good morning, Walter," Breanna said, helping herself to a fat strawberry from a bowl on the table.

"Lady Breanna." He gave her a quick smile. "Your uncle and your betrothed have gone—"

"Hunting." She bit a chunk out of the strawberry. "Yes, I know. I watched them leave."

"Ah." He cleared his throat. "Would it be unseemly for me to ask what you think of him, my lady? Sir Ansell, I mean."

She regarded him with surprise. "Yes, Walter, it probably would, but I'll answer you anyway. I'm not quite sure what to think."

He grunted. "Aye, well, 'tis early days yet."

"What do you think of him?"

"'Tis not for me to say."

"It was not for you to ask either, but you did. So, tell me what you think."

"Very well. He's a little too self-assured for my liking."

"Arrogant?"

"Aye, somewhat."

"Well, I appreciate your honesty. Not much I can do about it though, is there?" She finished off the strawberry. "Have you seen my aunt today?"

"Nay. She's unwell, apparently, and has not left her bed."

Thinking back to their exchange the previous evening, Breanna felt a pinch of concern. "Oh, dear. I'll look in on her later."

"I'm sure she'd appreciate that." Walter cleared his throat. "You should know, my lady, that we had an incident last night."

A fresh strawberry stopped on the way to her mouth. "What happened?"

"Well, it seems Arthur, Ansell's younger brother, had a bit of a scuffle with young Flip."

"A *scuffle*?" Breanna shook her head. "What does that mean? Arthur is a full-grown man. Flip is just a child. Why would they scuffle?"

Walter grimaced "Things got a wee bit unruly after you left," he said. "A lot of drinking and such. It seems Arthur took himself off to the stables with one of the kitchen maids, and they went up into the hayloft, where Flip was sleeping."

Breanna's blood ran cold. "And?"

"And, it seems Arthur told the lad to leave, and Flip refused. Or, at least, said something that angered the man."

Breanna gripped the edge of the table. "Please don't tell me he harmed the child."

"Not seriously." Walter drained whatever was in his goblet. "But he struck him, apparently, and all but tossed him out of the loft."

Breanna gasped. "Oh, Walter, nay. Where is Flip now?"

"Still in the stable, I think." Walter sat back. "And here's the irony of it. 'Twas Cedric who heard the commotion and stepped in to protect the lad. Got a punch in the nose for it."

Breanna gasped and rose to her feet. "And my uncle has allowed this man to stay at Ghyllhead?"

Walter shrugged. "Arthur admitted to being somewhat the worse for wear and apologized for his conduct. Your uncle had little choice but to accept it. He couldn't very well take the lad's side, could he?"

"I don't see why not." Breanna shook her head. "I'm going to see him."

The murmur of voices came from the hayloft. Breanna hoisted her skirts and climbed the ladder. "Flip? Where are you?"

"He's here, my lady." Cedric's head popped up from behind a pile of hay.

Ducking to avoid the low rafters, she made her way over. "How is—? Oh, Flip."

The boy lay curled up on his blanket, one eye bruised and swollen. "I'm all right," he said, with a sniff.

"You don't look it, little knave," Breanna replied, adopting Gabriel's nickname for the boy as she knelt at his side. "What did you say to him?"

Flip pouted. "Just that this was where I always slept."

"And he hit you for that?"

Cedric grimaced. "The man was drunk, my lady."

"Not an acceptable excuse." Breanna regarded her

uncle's young squire, noting the traces of blood around the edges of his nostrils. "I hear you came to his defence, Cedric. That was brave of you."

The squire's cheeks reddened a little. "No one's allowed to beat the lad but me," he said, with a half-smile. "Isn't that right, Flip?"

"Aye." Flip sat up.

"If Gabriel was here…" Breanna murmured, lifting a lock of Flip's hair from his forehead.

Flip sniffed. "I wish he was."

Cedric nodded. "So do I."

Breanna looked at the squire in surprise. "I thought you didn't like him."

He shrugged. "I thought him overly pious, my lady, but I've never seen anyone swing a sword like that. I enjoyed the training."

"There's more to knighthood than swinging a sword, Cedric."

"Aye." He grinned. "But I reckon swinging a sword is the best part."

Breanna chuckled. "Stay out of the way today, Flip, and rest. All right? I'll come and see you again later."

The boy nodded. "When are those men leaving?"

"Tomorrow morning."

"Good," he said. "I don't like them."

Breanna paused at the door to Linette's chamber, knuckles poised in readiness to knock. She wasn't quite sure what to expect from her aunt. She wasn't even sure how she felt at that moment. She ought to be angry at what had been said the previous night.

Resentful, at least. But somehow, Breanna only felt compelled to make peace. There'd been enough upheaval in her life of late, and she simply did not wish to deal with anymore.

She knocked, received a mumbled reply, and entered.

"Good morning, my lady." The smell of lavender didn't quite mask another, sickly smell that hung in the air. Linette lay on the bed, propped up against her pillows, a bowl on her lap. "I heard you were unwell, and thought I'd come to check on you."

Linette, whose colour matched the whiteness of her sheets, closed her eyes briefly. "I'm not in the mood for arguing, Breanna."

"Neither am I." She approached the bed. "I came to make peace, actually. Our confrontation last eve is bothering me."

"Why?" Linette looked her up and down. "Because you know what I said to be true?"

"Please don't." Breanna perched on the edge of the bed. "It doesn't really matter what I believe. Gabriel is not here anymore, nor is it likely I'll ever see him again, so whatever he did or did not do is no longer important." Just uttering the words created a weight in Breanna's chest that pressed down on her heart. "I have no wish to fight with you, my lady. Besides, I'm sure it can't be good for the child."

Linette looked down at her belly. "Winifred said the sickness should be gone by now, yet I still have it. Morning and night."

"I'm sorry. It must be tiresome."

"It is, as you'll soon find out."

Breanna forced a smile, though the thought of laying with Ansell—or any man she had no feelings for—created a knot in her belly. Yet women in arranged marriages did it all the time. She knew, of course, that love could grow out of such arrangements. She wondered if she would ever come to love Ansell.

"Do you love my uncle?" No sooner had she spoken the words than she gasped. "Oh, my lady, forgive me. I cannot believe I said that. It came out of nowhere."

Linette huffed. "You always were outspoken."

"Aye. 'Tis a failing of mine, I'm afraid."

A shout from the bailey drifted into the room, followed by the familiar clank of the portcullis rising. It was, for Breanna, a welcome diversion. She rose from her bedside perch. "It sounds like the men are back from the hunt, so I suppose I should make myself visible. Is there anything I can get for you, my lady? Anything you need?"

Linette shook her head and set her bowl aside. "I'm feeling a little better," she said. "You can tell Savaric I'll be down shortly."

"As you wish." She headed for the door.

"Are you in love with the Templar, Breanna?"

The answer came swiftly to her mind, which is where she left it. "Like I said, such things are of little consequence, my lady," she replied. "He's not here anymore."

"'Twas a fine chase." Grinning, Ansell tossed the fox tails onto the table. "Got two of the little bastards!"

Breanna gasped, her hand flying to her throat as she looked at her uncle. "Where were they caught?"

"A few miles west of here," Savaric said, giving her a reassuring smile. "I don't think you have any reason for concern, my dear."

"Ah, yes." Ansell flopped down in the seat beside her and reached for the wind jug. "I heard about your little friend. I should like to meet him."

Breanna regarded the two severed fox tails lying on the table and decided to ignore the comment.

"Where is your brother, sir?" she asked instead.

Ansell lolled back in his seat. "The stable, I think. Why?"

Breanna shrugged. "I understand there was an incident last night, and I confess to being a little concerned for—"

"If you're referring to the boy," Ansell said, "my brother was drunk and has since apologized for his behaviour."

"He has indeed, and sincerely too," Savaric said, giving her a warning glare. "I was thinking, it might be nice for you to take Ansell to meet Father Dunstan this afternoon, Breanna."

Breanna frowned. "I don't really see the point, uncle. The wedding is to be at Sir Ansell's home. Not here."

"Even so." Savaric's eyes narrowed a little. "It will give you some time to get to know each other a little better.".

"I agree." Ansell leaned forward and placed a hand over hers. The man had dried blood on his fingers and smelled of dog. "I would be honoured to meet this priest and see your church, my lady."

The thought of a cloistered life was becoming more attractive to Breanna with every breath she took. Then again, maybe she was just tired and, consequently, being unreasonable.

"Then we'll go," she said, finding a smile from somewhere. "Weather permitting, of course." She sent up a quick and silent prayer for rain.

The prayer was not heard, but a diversion came in the unexpected arrival of Lord de Clifford and some of his men, who strode into the hall toward the end of the meal.

"Lord de Sable, forgive the intrusion." De Clifford cast an eye along the head table. "We were in the vicinity so I took the opportunity to stop by, but it is perhaps not a good time."

"A good a time as any, my lord." Savaric gestured with his hand. "This is Sir Ansell Talbot, and his brother, Sir Arthur. Ansell is betrothed to my niece and is simply here for a visit. Gentlemen, this is Lord Robert de Clifford, Warden of the Marches and Marshal of England. Perhaps you've met already."

"Mathias' sons," de Clifford said, nodding a greeting. "Aye, I know your father well enough. I've met your elder brother too. Aldus. Is that his name?

He's not with you?"

"Nay, my lord," Ansell replied. "Aldus is staying with friends in Essex for the summer."

"Ah, I see." Smiling, De Sable approached Breanna. "My lady," he said, reaching for her hand and bowing over it. "'Tis a pleasure to see you again."

"Likewise, my lord," she said. "Do you have news for us?"

"Nothing definitive, I'm afraid. We have one or two leads, though, that I feel are worth investigating further."

Ansell leaned forward. "You are referring to the attack on the village, Lord de Clifford?" he asked.

"I am."

"What leads do you have?"

"I am not yet at liberty to elaborate, sir," de Clifford replied. "I'm sure you understand."

"Indeed." Ansell sat back. "I pray they bear fruit, my lord."

De Clifford grunted. "We do know who was responsible for the attack on the Templar knight, however."

It took a moment for the possible meaning of his words to register in Breanna's brain, and a cold hand squeezed her heart, halting it.

Savaric, looking puzzled, shook his head. "Forgive me, my lord. I confess I know nothing of this attack."

"Which Templar knight?" Breanna heard the question and knew it had come from her mouth, yet it seemed to have been spoken be a separate entity.

De Clifford frowned. "You were not informed of

the incident? Then I must beg your pardon, Savaric. I thought for sure you must have been aware. I speak of Sir Gabriel, the Templar knight who rescued Lady Breanna. He was attacked on his way to Furness. Four men set upon him, and I regret to inform you that he was—"

Breanna's agonized cry echoed off the walls. She fought to breathe and grabbed at air, trying to stop the dizzying slide into the pit that had opened up beneath her. She could not. Uttering a second cry more anguished than the first, she plunged into blackness.

Chapter Nineteen

"Out!" Linette's voice filtered through the darkness. "All of you. Out now."

There followed the mumbling of a man's voice and the sound of a door closing. Then something cool and damp pressed against Breanna's forehead.

She fought an urge to open her eyes. She felt safe, here in the darkness, hiding from a truth she couldn't bear to contemplate. But her fight to remain hidden failed. Consciousness pulled at her, bringing her up into the light.

"Gabriel?" His name scraped from her dry throat. *Oh, dear God.*

"Hush." Linette's voice. The cool dampness left her forehead, only to return a moment later. "It's all right."

Her eyes flicked open and met Linette's. "Where am I?"

"In your chamber," her aunt said. "You fainted. Don't try to sit up. Just lie still for a moment."

"Now I know why I never heard from him." She closed her eyes as a sob rose up like a stone in her throat. "Oh, Gabriel. I'm so sorry."

Linette's hand touched hers. "He's not dead, Breanna."

Her eyes flew open and searched her aunt's face for any sign of deception. Surely, she would be so cruel as to jest about this. "But Lord de Clifford said—"

"You fainted before he could finish." Linette removed the cloth from Breanna's forehead, dipped it into a bowl of water, and squeezed it out before replacing it again. "Gabriel was gravely wounded, but is apparently now recovering at the abbey." Her brow creased. "At least, that's the last news de Clifford had. And I must believe, given Gabriel's strength and God's good grace, that he will continue to recover. Can you believe he killed three of the men who attacked him? And the fourth died from an injury soon after. They were mercenaries, apparently, allegiant to no lord, though they were known to de Clifford as troublemakers. There'll be no repercussions, of course, since Gabriel was defending himself. So, you see, you have no need to mourn him, Breanna. He lives."

The immense sense of relief pushed fresh tears to Breanna's eyes. "Thank God. I swear I have never felt anything so horribly… final. I'm not sure if I would have survived knowing he was gone. Knowing that I'd never see him again."

Linette perched on the edge of the bed. "Your future husband was a little perturbed by your response to the news. I don't think he quite understood why you reacted so profoundly. Nor did de Clifford, in truth. Savaric told them some tale about you holding Gabriel in high esteem because of how he rescued you. I'm not sure Ansell quite believed it, though."

Breanna didn't care what they thought. Still drunk on relief, she drew a breath. "All this has made me realize something, my lady."

"And what is that?"

"I cannot marry Sir Ansell Talbot. I can give my

heart to no man, in truth."

Linette blinked. "You don't have to give him your heart, Breanna. Just your obedience and your virtue. In this, I fear you have little choice. The contract is binding."

"I do have a choice. You mentioned it yourself when I first learned of the betrothal."

Linette gave a soft laugh. "Nay, you cannot mean it. You've had a shock. Your thoughts are unclear."

"My thoughts are as clear as they have ever been." Breanna hoisted herself up onto her elbows. "Please understand. This is not something I ever wanted for myself, but it is preferable to the alternative. And, as you have pointed out, I have little choice."

"But a convent, Breanna?" Shaking her head, Linette rose to her feet. "I do not see you being happy trapped within the confines of such a place. And neither will Savaric, I warrant."

"Like I said, it is preferable to the alternative."

"And, like I said, you've had a shock." Linette picked up the bowl and started toward the door. "You need to rest for a while. I'll be back later, by which time I'm certain you'll have come to your senses."

"Aunt?"

"Yes?"

"Thank you for your kindness."

A flush of pink came to Linette's cheeks. "I'll be back in a while. In the meantime, I suggest you think on things further and straighten out your head."

Breanna's announcement that she'd decided to retreat to a convent had been greeted with about as much enthusiasm as a snowstorm in June.

Savaric had tried reason at first, his patience thinning as Breanna had remained steadfast. Ansell had done quite the opposite. In the beginning, he'd barely been able to hide his anger but appeared to gather himself and left Ghyllhead on a calm note.

It helped that, in the end, Linette suggested Breanna be granted permission to enter the convent simply for a period of meditation and reflection. Since the wedding was planned for the end of August, it would make little difference to allow her such a concession. Breanna agreed, though only to appease her uncle. In her mind, she still had no intention of marrying Ansell.

"A month, then," Savaric had said, nigh on spitting the words from his mouth. "More than enough time for the silly lass to see sense."

Breanna had chosen to retreat to St Bees priory, partially because it was not too far from Ghyllhead, but mostly because her mother had gone there.

"History repeating itself," Savaric had grumbled, to which Breanna had pointed out that she wasn't likely to be running away from the convent to marry a Scot.

So, letters requesting permission had been sent, responses received, and now, a mere sennight later, the day of departure had come. Breanna had bid all farewell, saving her last moments at Ghyllhead for Flip.

"Everyone keeps leaving," the boy said, his eyes bright with tears. "Sir Gabriel. You." He sniffed. "Mama."

God help me. Breanna's eyes filled as well. "I won't be gone forever, Flip. I just need some time to myself to think about things."

He shook his head. "You won't come back."

"I will, I swear it." Breanna crouched down to face him. "You'll be all right, little knave. Cedric is here, and Father Dunstan. I've talked to him about you, so you can speak to him if you need to. And I want you to keep yourself clean and eat properly. Promise me you will."

The boy heaved a sigh. "I promise."

"We're ready, my lady," Alfred said, from the doorway.

Breanna nodded, and dropped a kiss on the boy's cheek before she straightened. "Be good," she said. "And no spying on people."

The rugged nature of the Cumberland landscape always added time to a journey. It took a day and a half to reach the priory, with a night spent in a small, roadside inn. They—Savaric, Alfred and Breanna— each had a horse. There had been no need for a wagon, since Breanna had purposely brought few belongings. Several hours in the saddle, however, had her quietly wishing for an easier mode of transport.

She was glad when their destination at last came into view.

The priory of St Bees sat atop a cliff overlooking the Irish Sea at the spot where St Bega had apparently come ashore from Ireland. Consequently, it was said to be a place of miracles. Seeing it stirred Breanna's memories of Gabriel standing in a patch of sunlight, listening to Father Dunstan telling the story of the saint.

He was forever in her thoughts, of course. Breanna now knew why he hadn't written, but also realized he'd since had time to do so. The fact he hadn't seemed to imply he'd found his path, one separate from hers. Now she needed to find hers as well.

"I shall return a month from today. I want you to think hard about what you want, Breanna, and I pray it will not be this." Savaric glanced up at the sandstone walls of the priory. "You are not made for this. Ansell will be a good husband for you, a man worthy of you. You're fortunate he's still willing to take you as his bride, given all that has occurred."

He looked tired, Breanna thought, and a sudden surge of guilt caught her unawares. He'd said little as they'd travelled, though she'd felt his disappointment. She knew he wanted to see her wed, not because he wanted rid of her, but because he needed to know she'd be cared for and protected.

Savaric had been good to her. A father could not have treated her any better. Had she ever told him that? "I love you very much, Uncle," she said. "I'm grateful for all you've done, truly. God only knows where I'd be without you. It's just… I'm just so uncertain of everything right now. I'm hoping my time here will help me to see my way forward. That's all."

He grimaced as if in pain and looked away for a moment. "The Templar is gone, Breanna," he said, turning back to her. "He's not coming back. So, if you've come here looking for miracles, I'm afraid you'll be sorely disappointed."

That Savaric knew where her heart lay shocked her. "Not miracles, Uncle," she said. "Guidance, perhaps."

He drew breath, placed his hands on her shoulders, and pressed a kiss her forehead. "I love you too. I'll return in a month. And may God give you the answers you seek."

"I understand you're settling in quite well," the abbess said. "Sister Brigitte tells me you do not object to hard work and you observe all our liturgies She also mentioned your kindness to those among us who are less able than yourself."

Breanna had been at the priory for ten days. The waking hours passed quickly enough—she kept herself busy and involved with life inside the priory walls. The nights did not pass quite so easily, however.

"Everyone has been very kind to me, Reverend Mother."

The abbess smiled. "I'm glad to hear it. I'm not sure if you're aware, but your uncle told me of the attack on his village and your abduction. I understand those events have had a profound effect on you, which is hardly surprising. I pray your stay at St Bees will help to clear your mind of the fears that still reside there."

Breanna nodded. "Yes, I saw the letter he wrote to you. 'Tis certainly helpful to distance myself from reminders of that day."

Not quite the entire truth, but not a lie either.

"I'm sure it must be. Now then. Given what I've heard about you, I think you'd be suitable for a rather special undertaking. Nothing difficult. It simply means spending time with one of our sisters for an hour or two each day."

"Certainly, Reverend Mother. I'd be happy to."

"Excellent," she said, rising. "In helping others, we often end up helping ourselves Please follow me."

"May I know about her?" Breanna asked.

"Her name is Sister Agatha." The Abbess' robes rustled as she strode along the corridor. "She's been here for many years. Her mind is not her own, I'm afraid, although she's not at all dangerous. Quite the contrary, in truth. All you have to do is sit and talk to her, or read passages from the bible. You may see her mouth moving as if in prayer, but she makes no sound. Talk to her anyway. I make sure she has company every day. I believe it helps to stimulate her mind, what's left of it. That said, don't expect too much of a response."

Breanna frowned. "Can she hear?"

"Yes, though she shows no indication of it."

"What might I talk about?"

"Anything you like that befits her station and the sanctity of our order."

"Does she ever go out?"

"Not very often." The abbess stopped in front of a small, arched doorway. "On sunny days, she likes to sit and sew by the open window. Her eyesight is not what it was, so the sunlight helps her to see." She lifted the latch and pushed the door open. "Here you are."

Breanna stepped into a small room, blinking at the shock of brightness within. Afternoon sunshine poured through a small open window and reflected off walls as white as chalk. The only adornment, a small wooden cross, hung over the head of a narrow bed similar to Breanna's own. A small table and two plain wooden chairs occupied the spot beneath the window. A similar table, holding a jug, a washbowl, and another small bowl filled with herbs, stood against the adjacent wall. The scent of the herbs didn't quite smother the odour of urine.

A small hunched figure, her pale habit yellowed by time, occupied one of the chairs. Head bent over the table, she appeared engrossed with whatever held her attention.

"I've brought someone new to sit with you, Sister Agatha," the abbess announced. "Her name is Breanna."

The nun neither replied nor showed any awareness of her visitors.

"She's embroidering again." The abbess' expression softened. "She creates the same design over and over. It never varies. We don't know why, and we've never been sure what it represents."

Breanna raised her brows. "How unusual."

"Indeed. Oh, and please don't touch her. She doesn't like to be touched. Just sit and talk to her as she's working. She'll hear you."

Breanna nodded, wondering what, under Heaven, she might talk about. "How long shall I stay with her, Reverend Mother?"

"Till the bell rings for Nones, at which time you should pray with her or recite a psalm. You may leave after that if you wish." The abbess gestured to the empty chair. "Go ahead and seat yourself, child. There's naught to fear."

As the abbess left, Breanna slid into the chair and cocked her head to peer at the nun. She'd conjured up an image in her mind; that of a wizened old woman, with thin translucent flesh and gnarled hands. How wrong she had been. Looking at this woman was like gazing upon the face of an angel. Framed by a white wimple, the woman's features, lit by sunlight, reminded Breanna of a saintly statue one might find in church. Despite the etchings of time, Sister Agatha's countenance seemed to have been carved by master's hand, its grace and beauty still evident.

A faint blush of pink dusted each pale cheek. In contrast, thick, dark lashes fringed her eyes, which were currently downcast and focused on a small scrap of fabric clasped in a slender hand. The lines around her eyes and mouth hinted at a life of sorrow rather than joy. Her lips were moving, but she made no sound.

A sad angel.

Breanna leaned in a little closer and placed her hands atop the table. "Good day to you, Sister Agatha," she said. "My name is Breanna Glendenning. 'Tis a lovely day, is it not? I can smell the sea on the air. Can you?"

The woman lifted a skein of blue silk from a small basket on the table and set about threading a needle. Beside the basket sat a small wooden chest, crudely made, its metal catch rusted. Breanna wondered, vaguely, what it held. Then she leaned in further, trying to see Sister Agatha's work, but caught only a glimpse of it as the old nun recoiled. Heeding the Mother Superior's warning about the lady's aversion to being touched, Breanna sat back, her curiosity about this lady growing.

She fidgeted and cleared her throat. "Mother Superior said you like to embroider. I confess I do not, particularly. I like to write, though. And draw."

Breanna watched for any hint of a reaction, but saw none. She chewed on her lip, wondering if this troubled soul could actually hear anything at all. If so, she showed no sign of it.

She's been here for many years.

How many was many? And how long had the poor woman's mind been sealed like a tomb? It surely hadn't always been like that. Something terrible must have occurred to cause such a mental injury. Years of monastic seclusion hadn't cured it, either. Then again, maybe the seclusion had allowed her to live without fear.

Fidgeting again, Breanna glanced about the small room and wondered if she could ever commit to such a disciplined life. Since she did not wish to marry, she supposed she had little alternative. Despair reared its gloomy head.

"I'm not a nun, Sister Agatha." Breanna wrinkled her nose. "At least, not yet. I'm here because I..." She frowned as a lie teetered on the tip of her tongue—or a distorted version of the truth, at least. But it occurred to her that she didn't have to embellish her situation to Sister Agatha. She was free to share the raw truth with this sad, silent soul, since none of it would be spread beyond these walls.

She drew breath. "I'm here because I refused to marry a man I can never love, and also because the man I *do* love is someone I can never have. Firstly, because he's poor. He has no lands or wealth, so I would never be allowed to marry him, no matter how much I love him. I cannot fathom such logic, can you? It seems unfair that others should decide with whom we women must spend our lives." A sigh escaped her. "But his lack of wealth is not the only reason I cannot be with him. The truth is, he's taken holy vows. He's a Templar knight, you see. Or, at least, he was." Tears welled in her eyes. "He was gravely injured in an attack and taken to Furness Abbey, where he's to become a monk. I've been told he's still alive, and he must be, because I cannot bear to believe otherwise. Anyway, I'm here because I have no wish to marry anyone right now, and because I'm not certain what is to become of me."

The woman blinked and fished around in her basket for a moment before pulling out a skein of green thread. She then cut the blue with a small pair of scissors and proceeded to thread the needle with the green.

Breanna scrubbed a tear from her eye and leaned in a little closer. "May I see what you're making, Sister?"

The nun recoiled again.

"Forgive me." Breanna sat back. "I wasn't going to touch. I just wondered if you'd show it to me, that's all."

Still no response. Breanna heaved another sigh and glanced about again, allowing her mind to wander. Her gaze wandered outside. The window faced the south wall of the church and its arched stained-glass windows. Between lay a wide expanse of grass and clover, currently being mown by a tethered goat. Seeing that creature reminded Breanna of another, and her heart gave a painful lurch.

"I have a rather special friend named Theo, Sister Agatha," she said, and then proceeded to recount the entire story of how she'd met the fox. "He's never trusted men." Frowning, she nibbled on a fingernail. "Well, that's not quite true. He tolerates Father Dunstan, and he likes Gabriel very much. He's the

Templar knight I spoke of earlier." She lowered her gaze. "Gabriel Fitzalan. The man who has my heart. In fact, that's how we first met. 'Twas Theo who brought him to me when I was—" Breanna snapped her gaze to the nun, who'd made an odd little choking sound. "Are you all right, Sister Agatha?"

Eyes wide and fixed, the nun stared at the sewing needle grasped in her hand and then set it down. Her lips were parted slightly and the pink flush on her cheeks had vanished, leaving her pale and gaunt. With every passing moment, the woman seemed to grow older, wilting like a flower, a horrific impression that chilled Breanna's blood.

"Sister Agatha?" She placed a hand on the woman's arm. "What's wrong? Shall I fetch—?"

The inhuman cry that tore from the nun's throat was unlike anything Breanna had ever heard. Startled, Breanna echoed the cry with one of her own, crossing herself as she shot to her feet. Was the woman having a fit? Some kind of apoplexy?

The woman let out another agonizing wail and in a single, violent move, swept everything off the table. "He lied," she said, rising to her feet, her wild gaze fixed on Breanna. "He *lied*." Then, turning away, she stumbled over to her bed, and dropped to her knees.

Breanna whimpered and reached for the door, only to stagger back as it swung open. The abbess dashed into the room, her eyes widening as she saw the mess.

"What, in Heaven's name...? Oh, Breanna, what have you done?"

"Nothing," Breanna cried, her legs trembling so much she could hardly stand. "I did nothing at all, Reverend Mother. I was telling her about Theo, and all of a sudden, she—"

"Did you touch her?"

"Well, y-yes, but not until—"

"Oh, my dear! After what I told you." The abbess gestured to the open door. "Leave. Now."

Breanna gasped. "But, I didn't—"

"Leave, I said." A flush darkened the abbess' face. "Go to the church and wait for me there."

Breanna opened her mouth to argue again, but the abbess had already turned to crouch at Sister Agatha's side. Breanna heard her mutter something to the nun, who continued to whimper like a beaten child.

Still trembling, and with a sob in her throat, Breanna moved toward the door again, lifting her skirts to step over the objects scattered across the floor. She looked down at the small, wooden chest, its lid gaping open… and paused. The contents—dozens of pieces of embroidery— had spilled out. Most were folded, but some, in the chaos, had fallen open, the design on each one identical.

She creates the same design over and over.

And Breanna had seen it before.

The hair on her scalp lifted as a memory stirred. It brought with it an utterly implausible connection. A suspicion so ludicrous that she almost laughed. It had to be a coincidence, surely. From where she stood, it was impossible to make out the smaller details of the embroidery. She needed to see it more closely.

Casting a furtive glance at the abbess, she stooped to pick up one of the pieces, hiding it in the folds of her skirts as another nun rushed into the room.

"I heard a cry. What is…?" The nun took in the scene, her eyes widening. "Oh, Reverend Mother!"

Breanna fled.

As bidden, she went to the church and found a quiet corner at the back, beneath a small lancet window. Satisfied no one had noticed her, she opened the piece of fabric and lay it across her palm, tilting it toward the light.

There could be no doubt. The colours were brighter, but the little saintly figures, the colours, each intricately embroidered piece, were identical to the ones she'd seen on Gabriel's sample. "The rose window," she murmured, touching the raised threads with a fingertip while trying to fathom the consequences of what this discovery might mean.

Sister Agatha's reaction came when I had mentioned Gabriel's name. Surely, then, it cannot be a coincidence.

Gabriel's words came back to her. *"I don't even know where her body rests because my father refused to tell me."*

"Maybe he didn't tell you because your mother was not dead, Gabriel," Breanna whispered, her stomach churning. She prayed for it to be true. More than anything, she wanted it to be true.

Still, she had to find out more about Sister Agatha—where the woman had come from and under what circumstances. Had she always been weak-headed? Fearful and withdrawn? Most importantly, what was her real name?

Please, God, let it be Janette.

The murmur of voices pulled Breanna from her musing, and she glanced over to see the Mother Superior standing with two other sisters, all of them looking around the church.

There was little point in her hiding any longer. She folded the scrap of fabric and closed her fingers around it as she stepped out from her corner. "Are you looking for me, Mother Superior?"

The abbess spun round. "Ah, there you are, child. Yes, I wish to speak with you in my chamber." The woman appeared more shaken than angry, and a sudden fear grabbed Breanna. Had the woman succumbed?

"How is Sister Agatha?"

"Calmer," the abbess replied. "But I need to know what you said to her."

Breanna heaved a quiet sigh of relief. "I have questions too, Reverend Mother," she said, as they entered the abbess' chamber.

"Sit." The abbess gestured to her desk as she closed the door. Breanna did so, first waiting till the abbess did likewise.

"Reverend Mother, I—"

"What happened in there, Breanna?" The woman leaned forward and folded her hands atop the desk. "Tell me exactly what took place. I want to know what you did and what you said."

"I did nothing, Reverend Mother. I talked to her. That is all."

"Then you'll me what you said."

"Very well." Breanna shifted in her chair. "But you should know that some of what I told her was... is confidential."

The woman regarded her for a moment. "Are you saying you *confessed* to Sister Agatha?"

"I suppose." Breanna shrugged. "Though I do not consider what I told her to be an admission of sin. 'Twas merely a sharing of what lies in my heart. Things I have not shared with anyone else. Except God, of course."

"And now you will share them with me." To Breanna's surprise, tears welled up in the abbess' pale eyes. "I would know what you said to her, Breanna. I would know what you said to a woman who has never smiled, never wept, and who has spoken to no one but God for twenty-three years. A woman who is now on her knees, weeping and laughing, declaring it was all a lie. That he still lives. Over and over she says it, without pause. What does she mean? What lie? Who still lives?"

Breanna looked down at the scrap of embroidery still clutched in her hand. "Please, Reverend Mother, before I say anything, I would know the lady's story. Without knowing it, my answers to your questions would be based on supposition rather than certainty." She lifted her gaze. "Firstly, what is her real name?"

The abbess shook her head. "I cannot tell you that, because she has never told us. We found her on the steps of the priory one winter's night in a state much as you saw her today. We have long held the opinion that someone left her there, since she seemed to have no knowledge of where she was or how she got there. She would not speak and cried out in fear if anyone touched her. All she did was pray, and even then, her words were silent. We tried everything to reach into what remained of her faculties, but nothing worked. That is, except for her embroidery, which seemed to imply she came from a noble background."

Breanna put the piece of fabric atop the desk and smoothed it out. "This."

"Yes, it has always been the same." The abbess frowned. "Do you know what it indicates?"

She nodded. "I do, Reverend Mother, because I've seen it before. 'Tis a depiction of a window from the Church of Our Lady in Paris."

The abbess let out a soft cry. "Tell me how you know this. Tell me *what* you know."

"I cannot know everything for certain," she replied, "but I'll tell you what I believe. I believe Sister Agatha is a lady by the name of Janette Fitzalan. Janette has a son who was told, many years ago, that his mother had died. The son carries with him a scrap of fabric with this same design embroidered upon it. It was given to him by his mother. The son's name is Gabriel. He's the Templar who found me in the forest after I escaped my captor. I mentioned his name when I was talking to Sister Agatha. And I told her…" Breanna swiped at an errant tear with the heel of her hand. "I told her I was in love with him."

The abbess stared at Breanna for a moment, and then glanced away as if pondering. "But, why would she say…" She turned questioning eyes back to Breanna. "Do you happen to know who told Gabriel his mother had died?"

Breanna nodded. "His father. Gabriel told me the man had a cruel nature. They had no love between them. He died many years ago."

"Cruel indeed," the abbess replied, "since I suspect he also told Gabriel's mother a similar lie about her son."

Breanna's hand flew to her face. "God have mercy. What kind of man must he have been to do such a thing?"

The abbess shook her head. "Where is Gabriel now, child? Do you know?"

"He's at Furness Abbey, Reverend Mother."

"For what reason?"

"He…" She smiled over the sudden tightness in her throat. "He intends to join the Cistercian order, but he was recently gravely injured in an attack. I've been assured he is recovering, but I'm not certain as to his health."

"I see." The abbess sighed. "Well, I must write to him, of course, although I confess the wording of such a letter will have to be carefully thought out."

"Perhaps I can help you with it," Breanna said.

She gave Breanna a sympathetic smile. "While you've been instrumental in bringing about this revelation, my dear, I think it best you distance yourself from the repercussions of it."

"Why?" Breanna demanded, straightening. "As you say, Reverend Mother, I am a part of this and should remain involved."

"'Tis your involvement which concerns me," the abbess replied. "You admit to having feelings for this man, a man of the cloth be it Templar or Cistercian. These feelings you have, then, are sinful and must not be acknowledged or encouraged. 'Tis best you keep yourself distant from Sister Agatha and anything to do with this proceeding from now on."

"Nay!" Breanna gripped the arms of her chair. "I know where Gabriel's heart lies, and I accept that it is not with me. I respect what he is. *Who* he is. Please, Reverend Mother, do not shut me out of this. I would see it through to its conclusion."

"I will not be swayed, child." The abbess rose, leaned over the desk, and picked up the piece of embroidery. "This matter is closed to you. You may go."

"But… this is unfair." Tears spilling down her cheeks, Breanna pushed herself to her feet. "And you are wrong! What I feel for Gabriel is not sinful. It is a gift from God. The sin is yours in seeing it as something wicked."

Sobbing, she turned and fled.

Chapter Twenty

The midday repast had finished, though Savaric still nursed a half-goblet of wine. Linette had taken herself off for a nap, as she often did these days. The child she carried—his son, he hoped—had not been easy on her so far. Not that he'd mind a daughter. But girls were difficult, irrational creatures, as he knew from experience.

His sister had defied their father and run off with a Scot. That had not ended well. And it seemed Breanna had inherited her mother's foolishness, refusing to marry Ansell, choosing instead to imprison herself with all the other women at St Bees priory. She'd been gone a fortnight already.

Savaric had never been a pious man. He'd never quite understood the desire to renounce all and spend a life devoted to faith. The mere thought made him shudder. Life was a gift to be enjoyed. And, for the most part, he enjoyed it. He wondered if Breanna had seen sense yet and set her feelings for the Templar aside. He also wondered if the Templar had set his feelings for Breanna aside, too.

Savaric wasn't blind. The mutual attraction between the two had been quite obvious, and not only to him. Linette had noticed it, as had Walter. Linette's claim that Gabriel had tried to ravish her was, of course, a complete fabrication—one borne out of jealousy of her young niece. Despite her beauty, or maybe because of it, Linette struggled with her self-worth. So, although Savaric had taken his wife's side, he had never doubted Gabriel's honour. The man, when challenged, hadn't even tried to lay blame at Linette's feet or demean her at all. Savaric smiled at the memory and swirled the wine in his goblet.

Voices at the doorway drew his attention. He looked up to see Lord de Clifford striding toward him.

"My lord," he said, rising. "Welcome."

"My thanks," De Clifford said, his expression grim. "May we speak in private, Savaric? It won't take long."

"Of course." Savaric frowned. "This way, my lord."

He led the way to his private chambers at the back of the Great Hall and closed the door behind them. "I take it you have news," he said, gesturing to a chair.

De Clifford nodded. "I do indeed," he said, as he sat. "But first, where is your niece?"

Savaric felt the first stirring of unease. "Breanna is staying at St Bees priory for the month, my lord."

De Clifford raised a brow. "May I know what prompted that?"

"She is uncertain about the marriage arrangement and requested time to consider." Savaric narrowed his eyes. "What is this about?"

De Clifford took a breath. "There are many things we investigate when trying to track down these outlaws. The reports we receive from victims like your niece are crucial to these investigations. One of the things we take note of is jewellery. Often, stolen pieces are reworked to hide their original identity, so we check with local goldsmiths to see if they've been asked to rework specific pieces. In your niece's case, we asked around about the ring she said had been stolen."

"And you found something?"

De Clifford nodded. "You won't like this."

Savaric gripped the arms of his chair. "Go on."

"A goldsmith in Hexham told us he'd reworked a ring matching the description of the one stolen from your niece." De Clifford cleared his throat. "He'd been asked to make a locket from the gold in the shape of a flower, with an engraved cross in the centre of it, and set with the garnet."

Savaric shook his head. "Forgive me, my lord, I don't—"

"I'm an observant man, Savaric. When I was here a fortnight ago, I noticed a piece of jewellery your niece was wearing." He gave a grim smile. "A locket. Need I explain further?"

"Jesus Christ." Savaric's blood ran cold. "Are you telling me that the locket Ansell Talbot gave Breanna was made from her mother's stolen ring?"

"Odious, isn't it?"

"He was one of the men who attacked the village?"

"Nay, Ansell Talbot had naught to do with the attack, but his elder brother, Aldus, did. Another observation from my visit the other week. Ansell said his brother was staying with friends in Essex." De Clifford tapped the side of his nose. "I decided to check that and found it to be false. In truth, no one had seen Aldus for several weeks. That's because the man fell from his horse and snapped his neck not long after he'd abducted your niece from St Bega's."

Savaric sat back. "Ansell confessed?"

"Nay, their father did," de Clifford replied. "It's amazing what a few days in a rat-infested dungeon will do. The truth is, Aldus was the only one actively involved in these illegal activities, though the family knew of them, which makes them equally as guilty in my book."

"But…" Savaric ran a hand through his hair. "Why, in God's name would he arrange a contract of marriage with Breanna?"

De Clifford grimaced. "Accidents happen. Suffice to say your niece has had two lucky escapes from this family."

"Are you saying they'd have *killed* her?"

"I don't think it was intended as a love match, Savaric. They apparently blamed her for Aldus's death."

"May God forgive me." Savaric tasted bile. "I'd have sent the girl to her death."

"Aye, well, you didn't." De Clifford rose. "I'll keep you informed as to the final outcome, but they'll hang, most likely."

Savaric stood. "I'd like to be there when they do," he said. "Christ, I'll pull on the damn ropes myself."

De Clifford smiled. "Go and get that niece of yours out of the convent, Savaric. The decision's been made for her."

Chapter Twenty-One

"Thank you." Gabriel brought Father Simon's hand to his mouth and kissed the ring "I owe you much, my friend."

"And I expect repayment, Gabriel," Father Simon replied. "I'd like it in the form of a letter that tells me you're safely arrived in Scotland."

"As you demand." Gabriel climbed into the saddle. "Perhaps, one day, you might find the time to visit us."

"Perhaps," he replied. "I confess to being intrigued by this church you speak of."

"You'll be made welcome, Father," Jacques said, already seated atop his horse. "You have my thanks as well. May God keep you."

"And you, Brother. Godspeed."

Gabriel looked back only once as they left, halting Kadar at the top of the hill to gaze down at the great abbey, its edges blurred by the mist that accompanied the dawn. He felt no regret. As much as his faith meant, he knew Ewan had been right. Knighthood was in his blood. To surrender it would be akin to losing an essential part of himself. As for the future, he'd entrust it to a higher power.

After an uneventful night in a Kendal inn, they continued on the next day, one blessed with warm summer breezes. As the afternoon waned, a familiar line of hills came into view and Gabriel felt the familiar ache beneath his ribs. He'd be glad once those hills lay behind him.

As they reached the crest of a small rise, the distant peal of a distant church bell rang out. Gabriel's chest constricted as he looked toward the familiar sound. He wondered how the old priest fared. He wondered what had been in Breanna's basket that morning. He wondered who had escorted her to and from the church.

"'Tis odd that the bell should ring just as we are passing," Jacques said, intruding into Gabriel's thoughts. "One might think we were being summoned."

Gabriel gave him an incredulous look. "I do not find it odd at all, given the hour. 'Tis obviously the bell for Nones."

"Ringing at St. Bega's, methinks," Jacques said, giving Gabriel a pointed look.

Gabriel grimaced. "How did you know?"

"Your bleak expression."

"Ah."

Jacques raised a brow. "So?"

"So what?"

"So, I kept my word. But now we're so close, I think we should visit this priest friend of yours."

"I think not."

"Why not?"

"Because there's no point." Gabriel bit down and urged Kadar onward. "She's not there."

"The priest is a woman?"

Gabriel gave him a withering glance. "You know what I mean."

Jacques huffed. "As you wish, but for what it's worth, I believe—" He frowned and halted his horse.

"Believe what?"

"That you're making a mistake, Brother," he said, and gestured to the road ahead. "Is that who I think it is?"

Gabriel followed his gaze and his hands tightened on the reins. "Nay," he muttered, his heart skipping a beat, "'tis not possible."

A little farther along, the trail passed beneath the leafy boughs of an ash tree, its broad shadow offering shelter and shade to travellers. It also marked the turn for St Bega's church... and Ghyllhead. Today, the spot beneath the tree's canopy was occupied by a familiar creature, who, for all the world, looked as though he was waiting for someone.

"Theo?"

The fox let out a yip, turned a circle, and vanished down the road toward Ghyllhead.

"Is it him?" Jacques asked.

"I think so, aye," Gabriel said. "Watch."

A moment later, the fox reappeared and repeated his ritual. Gabriel thought back to the first time he'd seen Theo, how he'd followed him into the woods.

How he'd been led straight to Breanna.

"Aye, it's him."

Jacques shifted in his saddle. "Seems obvious he wants you to follow him."

Gabriel looked over to where Ghyllhead lay, tucked down in the vale out of sight. "Aye, but it makes no sense," he said. "Unless..."

Unless Breanna never married.

"Well, Brother, you can stay here if you wish." Jacques gathered up his reins. "But I intend to find out what God is trying to tell us. Or more specifically, tell *you.*"

Gabriel watched Jacques ride away. He fully intended to follow, of course, but he needed a moment to prepare for what was to come. Not that he had any idea of what that might be. He glanced skyward. "Be merciful," he murmured. "I beg of you."

Kadar snorted and pawed the ground. Gabriel took a breath and pressed his heels to the gelding's sides.

He caught up with Jacques a short time later, still following Theo.

Jacques gave him a critical look. "If for no other reason, 'tis good that we are stopping, Brother," he said. "You look weary."

Gabriel didn't bother denying it. He would not be sorry to leave the saddle. At the same time, nothing to do with fatigue, his gut felt as though it had twisted into a knot.

Theo turned onto Ghyllhead's thoroughfare.

"Nay, Theo," Gabriel said, "we're going to the church."

The animal halted and watched as they went on their way.

He didn't follow.

By the time they reached St Bega's, the bell had ceased its toll. They dismounted, tethered their horses, and entered, the groan of the door bringing Father Dunstan out of the shadows.

"Good day, gentlemen," he said, rubbing his hands together is if trying to rid them of dust. "May I be of...?" He parted with a gasp and crossed himself. "Heaven help us. Gabriel, is that you?"

"It is, Father." He approached and took the priest's hand in his. "How are you?"

"Shocked, my son, to put it mildly." Father Dunstan raked a critical gaze over Gabriel. "But beyond pleased to see you looking so hale. We'd heard you'd been set upon and gravely wounded. What are you doing here?"

"We're on our way back to Scotland." Gabriel turned toward Jacques. "Brother Jacques Aznar, this is Father Dunstan."

Jacques extended a hand. "I've heard much about you, Father."

"All good, I hope, but..." The man blinked. "Forgive me, I'm not certain I heard you correctly. You're returning to Scotland?"

"Aye." Gabriel smiled. "I have come to realize that is where I belong, after all. My friends are in Scotland. My *home* is there."

"I see," he said, in a tone that implied the opposite. "And you have surrendered your mantles?"

"Temporarily," Jacques replied. "The risks have proven themselves to be too great."

"Ah, of course. I can understand that, given what you went through. A cowardly attack."

Gabriel drew breath. "How is Savaric?"

"Savaric is well." The priest gave a grim smile. "Though much has happened since you left, Gabriel."

"What do you mean?"

"Sit." Father Dunstan gestured to a bench. "And I'll tell you about it."

"There's no need," a voice bellowed from the doorway. "I'll tell him myself."

Savaric, Alfred and another henchman stepped into the church.

"Lord de Sable," Gabriel said. "'Tis good to see you."

Savaric nodded but said nothing for a moment. He glanced at Jacques, and then looked Gabriel up and down. "'Tis good to see you too, Templar." A glint came to his eye. "If that is truly what you are."

Gabriel smiled at the reference to their first meeting and answered accordingly. "What gives you cause to question it?"

"Your mantle is grey."

"Less conspicuous."

"It took a brush with death to make you realize that?"

"It seems I have a knack for failing to see the obvious." Gabriel gestured toward Jacques. "This is Jacques Aznar, a fellow knight of the Temple. Jacques, this is Lord Savaric de Sable."

Jacques nodded. "My lord."

"Templar." Savaric's gaze flicked from one to the other. "We're actually here to challenge you. You were seen from the battlements. Two horsemen, armed, heading for the village. The alarm was raised. We didn't even stop to saddle the horses. Then I recognize Kadar when I got here."

"My pardon," Gabriel said. "We should have stopped at the gatehouse first, though we didn't plan on staying for long."

Savaric grunted. "Did I hear you say you're on your way back to Scotland?"

Gabriel nodded. "You did, my lord."

"And are you in a hurry to get there?"

"Nay, my lord," Jacques replied, giving Gabriel a pointed look. "We're in no hurry at all."

"Good," Savaric said. "Because I need your help. Nay, don't ask. I'll explain everything back at Ghyllhead."

Gabriel had not quite been prepared for the emotional burden that came with his return. Flip had greeted him with undisguised enthusiasm, though the child's smile had faded when he'd learned the visit would not be a long one. Cedric and Hubald had given him a respectful greeting, Cedric telling him how he'd been practising some of the things he'd learned.

Walter had assumed his familiar smirk. "I had a feeling you'd be back," he said. "Your timing is perfect." The steward had not elaborated.

But Gabriel, sitting with Jacques in Savaric's private chamber, had just found out why. And it had turned his blood cold. "Are you telling me Breanna was promised to a man who would have *killed* her?"

Savaric nodded. "De Clifford is of that opinion, aye."

"Does Breanna know?"

"Nay." Savaric shifted in his seat. "I'd have left for the convent three days ago, but Linette is unwell and afraid for her child. I daren't leave her. Not right now. I'd like you to go, if you can spare the time. You'll be compensated, of course."

"Of course, my lord." Jacques said, before Gabriel could respond. "We'll leave at dawn. And compensation will not be necessary."

"Excellent. You'll need a letter of introduction for the Abbess. I'll see to it right away."

Chapter Twenty-Two

Breanna wiped her forearm across her brow and pushed a stretch into her back. It had been a warm day, though a soft breeze off the sea helped to keep the air sweet. She glanced down at the dark patch of earth, now freshly turned and free of weeds. The physical effort helped settle her nerves, but they continued to fray as the days passed.

Miracles were taking place and Breanna had been denied any and all involvement in them. She had pleaded several more times, but the abbess had remained steadfast in her decision. Breanna's fear was that Gabriel would come, and she wouldn't be allowed to see him. Worse, she might not even be told of his arrival. Or she might not even be there when he arrived. In another nine days, Savaric would be coming to collect her. Of course, she could always choose to stay.

Heaving a sigh, she collected up the garden tools and took them over to the rain barrel to wash them. Engrossed in her task, she didn't see the abbess approaching till her shadow announced her presence.

"Breanna, dear, it appears you'll be leaving us a little earlier than anticipated. Your uncle has sent an escort for you. Can you collect your things, please? They're waiting."

"An escort?" Breanna frowned. "I don't understand. Is something wrong?"

"Not precisely. According to the letter he sent, your betrothal contract has been annulled, and he wants you to return home."

"Annulled?" Breanna's stomach lurched. "Does he say why?"

"Nay, he does not, but the tone of his letter is not at all grave. Perhaps the knights he sent will be able to answer your questions. Go and collect your things. I'll not ask you again. They're waiting for you in the outer courtyard."

Confused and close to tears, Breanna did as bid. She stumbled into the outer courtyard expecting to see Alfred or Elwyn. But the sight that greeted her all but stopped her heart. Maybe she'd had too much sun and it had addled her brain. Or, the entire episode in the garden hadn't been real. Maybe her entire day thus far had been a dream. For she had to be dreaming now. She had to be.

"Gabriel?" Tears blurred her eyes and she scrubbed them away. It was definitely him, although he wasn't wearing his white mantle, she noticed. And he looked a little thinner, perhaps. But the mere sight of him was a balm to her soul. "What... what are you doing here?"

"It would seem God is willing, my lady," he said. Were they tears in his eyes as well?

"But... I don't understand." Breanna glanced briefly at a man who stood in silence behind Gabriel. A stranger. "Did you get the letter?"

"What letter?" Gabriel moved toward her. "We've come to escort you back to Ghyllhead, Breanna.

Savaric sent us." He glanced over his shoulder. "This is Jacques Aznar, my Templar Brother. I told you about him. Do you remember?"

"I… yes, I do. But what about…?" She shook her head. "Oh, God help me. I'm so confused."

"So it seems." He frowned. "I know this is unexpected, but I—"

"Did you tell the abbess who you are?"

"I told her we were your escort and gave her Savaric's letter. Why?"

Breanna absorbed the information. "Well, that explains why she left you here."

"Now I'm confused." He cupped her cheek. "What's going on, Breanna? Has something happened?"

"Yes." She placed her hand over his and laughed through her tears. "Yes, it has. And it's a miracle. A true miracle. Please wait here. I have to fetch the abbess."

"A miracle? What—?"

She stood on tiptoes and kissed him square on the mouth. "I love you, Gabriel. With all my heart. I need you to know that. Please. Just wait here."

Gabriel sat in the abbess' chamber and stared at the pieces of fabric spread out across the desk. "What is this?" Feeling slightly sick, he looked at the abbess and then at Breanna. "Where did you get these?"

"Do you recognize them, Gabriel?" the abbess asked.

"Yes, I recognize them. And I need to know where you got them."

"Sister Agatha made them."

"Sister Agatha." Gabriel picked up one of the pieces and studied it. His hand trembled. He knew every detail. Every colour. Every single stitch. He had looked upon the same design a thousand times. "Who is she?"

"We don't know for certain," the abbess said.

"I do." Breanna placed her hand atop his. "I know who she is. I knew it as soon as I saw that design. Would you like to meet her, Gabriel? She's been waiting a long time."

Gabriel swallowed. "So have I," he said. "God help me, Breanna, I'm terrified."

Breanna looked at the abbess. "May I?"

The woman heaved a sigh and nodded. "I'll be outside the door. Just in case."

"I'll wait with you if I may, Reverend Mother," Jacques said.

Gabriel pushed the door open, stepped into the room and held his breath.

She had the face of an angel.

Gabriel knew that to be so, for he'd once seen her likeness, carved in stone, gazing down at him in church. She only lacked the wings. He watched her now, her head bent over her work, lips moving in silent prayer. He supposed it didn't really matter as long as God could hear her. And she'd once told him God heard everything. Every prayer. Every thought. Since then, Gabriel had tried to keep his words and his thoughts kindly, and made sure to pardon himself for any transgressions.

"*Bonjour, Maman*," he said, using the language of her birth.

She looked up at him with a smile. "Ah, there you are, *mon petit*," she said. "I have been waiting for you. Sit, please, and tell me about your day."

Gabriel blinked away tears and pulled up a chair.

"It was as if he became possessed by the Devil." Gabriel swallowed bile. "He could enter a room and fill it with fear without speaking a single word. You could see the evil on his face. In his eyes. The way his mouth twisted. And the demon within him would always take it out on her. On my mother. She knew when it was coming. I did, too, though I was only little. She'd always send me out of the room, and I would run to mine and hide under my bed. But I would hear him. Hear his rage. And I would hear... I would hear her..." He closed his eyes and drew breath. "Christ help me."

"Gabriel, stop." Breanna slid her hand into his. "You don't have to do this. You don't have to tell us anymore. By God's good grace, your mother survived, and no one will ever harm her again. She's safe, and now that she's been reunited with her child, she's also happy. 'Tis a miracle that has come out of evil."

Gabriel brought Breanna's hand to his lips. "I stood up to him," he said. "Right before I was sent away to foster. I confronted him."

"And?" Jacques said.

"He beat me to within an inch of my life. And that hurt my mother more than anything he could ever have done to her. I realized, then, that she had always shielded me and protected me from the harm he might have done to me. Because of that, I swore I would always strive to protect those weaker, those who could not defend themselves."

"Like Flip?"

"Yes, Breanna." Gabriel heaved a sigh. "Like Flip."

They were seated in a quiet corner of the roadside inn where they would be spending the night before returning to Ghyllhead.

Gabriel's head still reeled from finding his mother alive. Even now, he could scarcely believe it. He'd spent several hours with her, telling her of his life, though when he'd asked about hers, she merely clucked her tongue and continued with her embroidery.

She knew him, certainly, and she heard all he'd said. But it was clear her mind had long since ceased to function normally. Part of it would, he suspected, be forever closed, guarding against the nightmares of her past.

One thing Gabriel's mind had accepted was the fact that he wanted Breanna in his life. How to achieve that, however, remained to be seen. He felt her gaze on him and met it. She loved him. She'd told him so. And even if she hadn't, he could see it shining in her eyes.

"I'm going to ask Savaric for your hand, Breanna," he said. "I'll not go back to Scotland without you."

"*Finalement*," Jacques said, smiling as he sat back. "Finally, he accepts the truth of what lies in his heart."

"Given what might have happened with Ansell, I don't think he'll say no," Breanna said. "And if he does, I shall simply do what Mama did and go anyway."

Chapter Twenty-Three

Gabriel made his wedding vows to Breanna on the steps of St Bega's church on a fine Saturday morning in August. Of all the vows he had taken, these meant the most to him. It had been a quiet service, with only Savaric, Jacques, and Walter in attendance. Well, that's if one did not count the brief appearance of a fox who emerged from the trees by the church and watched the proceedings for a while.

Linette sent apologies for her absence, blaming her continued delicate health, though Savaric hinted it might have been more due to what had—or had not—occurred in the scriptorium.

Gabriel didn't care. He only had eyes for his bride, who had daisies woven into her hair and whose sweet scent teased his senses. It had been an emotional service—holy and beautiful and miraculous. Yet bitter-sweet as well.

On the morrow, they would be heading to Scotland, leaving behind people they loved, some of whom they might never see again. For now, though, Gabriel put such thoughts aside. Tonight, he simply wanted to spend time with his wife.

His *wife*.

He couldn't help but smile. He'd expected Savaric to refuse his request to marry Breanna. After all, he had nothing of worth to offer. Just his protection, his loyalty, and his love. It had apparently been enough.

Then again, maybe Savaric knew that his niece's wild spirit would not accept any other response.

Now Breanna lay in Gabriel's arms, beautiful in her nakedness, sweet sounds of pleasure coming from her mouth as his hands moved over her. He lowered his lips to hers in a tender caress as his fingers sought out the wet heat of her centre.

She gave a soft cry of delight against his mouth and lifted her hips to his touch. Gabriel groaned and trailed his lips down her throat and over the rise of a pale breast, seeking the sensitive peak.

"Gabriel," she said, her voice pleading as she reached for him. He moved to cover her, the head of his cock replacing his fingers. Instinctively, she moved against it, lifting her hips, trying to draw him inside.

"I love you," he murmured and entered her with a single stroke.

She drew a sharp breath, and he waited, the sheer heat and tightness of her pushing him to the edge of climax. Then, at last, she moved beneath him, and the slow rhythm began, building as their pleasure intensified.

He felt her clench around him, heard her cry out his name as she lifted her hips, and the world around him shattered into a thousand pieces of light.

Chapter Twenty-Four

"Well?" Jacques shifted in his saddle. "Any regrets, Brother?"

Gabriel pulled in a lungful of sea air and glanced about. To the west, the skies over the Irish Sea had been set afire by the setting sun. To the east, the land stretched away to the line of distant mountains. Above, seabirds called to each other as they rode the incessant breeze on outstretched wings.

And directly ahead, Castle Cathan's grey walls rose up from their clifftop seat.

"Nay," Gabriel replied. "None at all. I'm where I'm supposed to be."

"'Tis exactly as you described," Breanna said. "More beautiful, even."

Gabriel caught the slight waver in her voice. "They'll love you," he said. "You'll see."

She wrinkled her nose. "I still think you should have told them we were coming. Given them some kind of warning."

Jacques huffed. "Absolutely not. I want to see Ewan's face when he realizes you've returned."

Gabriel looked over at Flip, who sat silent atop his black pony. Savaric had agreed to let the boy go too, following pleas from both Gabriel and Breanna. "What do you think, little knave?"

The boy nodded. "I like it."

Even at this distance, a man's face was visible peering over the castle's battlements. He stared at them for a few moments and then disappeared.

"I believe we've been spotted," Gabriel said.

No sooner had the words been spoken than the gates swung open and another man stepped forward, scratching his head.

"Duncan." Jacques chuckled. "He can't believe his eyes, I'll warrant."

As they drew ever closer, a third man appeared and stood at Duncan's side for a moment before striding forward.

Gabriel would have recognized him anywhere.

"Wait, Breanna," he said, halting Kadar and dismounting. She did so and slid into his arms when he reached for her. He took her hand and threaded his fingers through hers.

"Ewan?" she asked, watching the man approach.

"Aye." Gabriel gave her hand a gentle squeeze. "I want you at my side when I introduce you, not atop a horse."

Chest heaving, Ewan stopped a couple of strides away. He gave Jacques a nod, frowned at the sight of Flip, and then turned his attention to Gabriel and Breanna, glancing down at their joined hands. His eyes widened a little and the beginnings of a smile settled on his lips as he locked eyes with Gabriel.

For now, Gabriel remained silent. The introductions could wait a little longer. To speak at that moment did not seem appropriate, nor was it even necessary. That he was glad to see his friend did not need to be verbalized. Each knew how the other felt. Each knew the bonds of friendship and brotherhood had not been weakened by time and distance. Nor would they ever be.

Ewan nodded again, as if agreeing with Gabriel's thoughts. Then, with the glint of a tear in his eyes, he spoke at last. "Welcome home, Brother," he said, "and you too, my lady. Welcome home."

It had been a night of story-telling, a night of laughter and tears. There had been much to tell; a sharing of revelations and miracles. The hour was late, yet still they sat together in Ruaidri's chamber, reluctant to relinquish the joys of reunion.

Only young Flip had not endured. With his belly full of Glenna's oatcakes, he'd been given his own pallet in a cosy corner of the kitchen and was asleep before his head hit the pillow.

Ewan scratched his jaw and winked at Breanna. "I still cannae believe this wee lass agreed to marry you."

Gabriel lifted Breanna's hand to his lips. "There are times when I cannot believe it either," he said. "I confess, 'tis still something of a mystery, this… whatever this is that I feel. I have yet to understand it."

"What's to understand?" Ewan shrugged. "You'd die for her. 'Tis as simple as that."

Gabriel smiled. "A thousand times over."

"Heaven forbid you are ever called upon to do so," Breanna said. "I tried life without you and did not like it at all."

Ruaidri rose to his feet. "Aye, well, I think it's time we got some rest," he said. "We can continue this tomorrow."

"Agreed." Ewan rose and held out a hand to Cristie. "Come on, *mo chridhe*. You've done enough today."

"I've had the north chamber made up for you," Morag said to Gabriel and Breanna. "It hasnae been used in a good while, so it 'tis a wee bit makeshift for now, but that's because Jacques' letter failed to mention you were coming back." She scowled at Jacques, who chuckled.

"I wanted it to be a surprise," he said, "and it was worth it to see Ewan's face."

"I'm sure it'll be fine," Breanna said. "Thank you, Morag. And thank you too, Laird McKellar, for everything."

"You're welcome, lass," Ruaidri replied. "And I mean that sincerely."

Gabriel opened his eyes to a hint of dawn light and turned to look at Breanna, who lay curled up with her back to him. He rolled over and tucked her against him, giving a soft groan of approval at the way her bottom fit so perfectly against his groin.

"You're insatiable," she mumbled as he hardened against her.

"'Tis your fault," he replied, "you're irresistible."

She gave a soft chuckle and snuggled closer against him.

"Keep doing that, my lady," he said, nuzzling her hair, "and we'll be late for breakfast."

"Again?"

He laughed.

They'd been at Castle Cathan for almost a week, during which time they settled into something of a routine.

It had rained every day, which had delayed their visit to *Eaglais Chruinn*, the round church built for the Templars by Ewan's grandfather. Perhaps today, weather permitting, they might at last be able to visit the beautiful glen known as *Lorg Coise Dhé*, or God's Footprint. Gabriel was eager to show it to Breanna. He also looked forward to seeing its ancient guardian.

Fortunately, the skies cooperated and, after a late breakfast, they set out on horseback.

"It took ten years to build the church and Ewan's grandfather donated it to the Templars once it was finished," Gabriel explained, as they entered a patch of pine forest. "Father Iain is a Templar priest who served with Ewan's grandfather in the Holy Land."

Breanna gasped. "He must be ancient."

"He is."

Breanna fell silent for a few moments. "If the church belongs to the Templars, and the Templars no longer exist, then who—"

"The Templars still exist, Breanna," Gabriel said, frowning. "You're married to one."

"Of course. Please forgive me," she said, her voice subdued. "I meant no offence."

Gabriel felt an immediate stab of remorse and groaned. "Nay, my love, 'tis I who should beg forgiveness. Your question has merit, and to answer, I believe the church is meant as a refuge for those who seek shelter from persecution."

"An admirable function," she said.

"And not the only one."

"What do you mean?"

Gabriel smiled. "You'll see."

A short while later, they reined in their horses at the edge of the pine forest and looked down at the pretty little glen. And at its centre, the church, which sat in a beside a small, dark loch.

"Oh, Gabriel." Breanna shifted in her saddle. "It's beautiful. Like a little piece of Heaven! A perfect place to build a church."

"I don't disagree," he said, and led the way down the hill. "Come and meet its guardian."

Father Iain, clad in green robes and clasping a staff, appeared on the steps of the church as they drew near.

"He misses nothing," Gabriel said, halting Kadar and helping Breanna down.

Father Iain made no bones about his delight at seeing Gabriel, tears rising in his eyes as they so often did when people came to visit him.

"So, laddie, you couldnae stay away," Father Iain said, after the introductions had been made. "In truth,

I cannae quite understand why you left us in the first place, but seeing this bonny wee bride you've brought back, I'll concede England must have some virtues."

"I'm half Scottish, Father Iain," Breanna said, smiling.

The old priest chuckled. "I might have known." His expression sobered as he addressed Gabriel. "I hear our brothers face challenges south of the border too. I understand you were set upon simply because of the mantle you wore. I prayed for you, Brother."

Gabriel inclined his head. "It seems your prayers were heard, Father."

"I also heard those responsible didnae fare quite as well." The priest assumed a grim expression. "They should have known better than to mess with a warrior of Christ."

Gabriel decided not to respond to that and instead gestured to the church. "I'm going to show Breanna around, Father. With your permission."

"You don't need my permission," Father Iain replied. "Neither does your lady."

Gabriel led Breanna inside, watching her face as she took in the splendour of the place. "Oh," she said, turning a circle. "I don't believe I have ever seen anything quite so incredible. These carvings are magnificent."

"Created by master masons," Gabriel said. "Come. I'll show you where Ewan's grandfather lies."

"Ewan's father is here as well," Breanna observed a short while later as they stood by the effigies of the two knights.

"Aye, the Templars agreed to allow all the McKellar men to rest here if they wish." Gabriel gestured to the stained-glass window. "When the sun shines through, it casts the reflection of the cross onto the tombs."

"'Tis a very peaceful place," Breanna said. "I completely understand why Calum McKellar was compelled to build here."

Gabriel smiled. "There was a little more to Calum McKellar's vision than what you see here, Breanna." He slid his hand into hers. "Come. I'll show you *Eaglais Chruinn* greatest secret."

Breanna crouched down and plucked a sprig of white heather. "Heather grows in Cumberland too." She brought the sprig to her nose and inhaled. "But I don't recall ever seeing any colour but purple."

"There's a McKellar legend attached to the white flower," Gabriel said. "I forget the story, but Morag or Cristie will know of it, I'm sure. We'd best start back, my love. I don't like the look of that sky."

There were still times when Breanna couldn't quite grasp all that had occurred since the fateful attack on St Bega's. Being with Gabriel, feeling his love and protection, sharing his days and his nights, still overwhelmed her. They belonged together. Of that, she had no doubt at all. She had known it from the first day she'd met him. It had just taken a little while for their destinies to align.

Now, they rode through the pine forest in companionable silence, as much at ease with each other as at any other time. The scent of pine sweetened the air, and the shaded path lent itself to reflection. And indeed, Breanna reflected on the day and all she'd been privileged to witness. The church. The tombs of the McKellar knights. The white heather.

The secret vault, hidden beneath the altar.

It was no secret that the Order of the Temple possessed lands and churches and castles. Breanna had also heard tales of Templar treasure—secret hoards of precious metals and sacred artefacts—but she'd generally assumed them to be nothing more than fanciful rumours.

She now knew differently.

Gabriel and Ewan and Jacques had not left France empty-handed. Their boat had ferried more than men and horses and supplies. It had also been a treasure ship, laden with gold, silver, and holy artefacts that had been placed in their care.

Earlier that day, Gabriel had said that the Templars still existed. And, of course, they did. But more and more they were being driven underground, or absorbed into other religious military orders.

Or maybe some of them were living quietly among unsuspecting people, guarding secrets that would only ever be told to those trustworthy enough to keep them. Gabriel had honoured Breanna with his trust by allowing her to descend into the bowels of the church and witness one of those secrets.

"Nay, 'tis not possible." Gabriel's murmur broke into her thoughts. She glanced at him as he reined Kadar to a halt, his action prompting her to halt her mount as well.

"What's wrong?"

He gestured to the path ahead. "Look."

She did so, her heart skipping a full beat at the sight of a fox standing in the middle of the trail further along.

"Oh, nay, Gabriel." Breanna shook her head. "'Tis surely just a coincidence. He could not possibly have followed us all the way from—"

The fox gave a yip, wagged his bushy tail, and turned a full circle.

Epilogue

Jacques leaned against the wall of the armoury watching Hammett showing Flip how to clean mail. The young lad had potential. He was keen, obedient, and not without courage. He'd settled easily into his life in Scotland. As had Breanna. Then again, Jacques mused, Gabriel's lady had Scots in her blood.

And, three days ago, in an incredible demonstration of devotion, another of Ghyllhead's residents had shown up. Even now, Jacques shook his head thinking about the miles the little fox had done. It was beyond belief.

And as for Gabriel...

Jacques smiled as he thought of his friend. The man had been a Templar to the core; pious, brave, disciplined. Compassionate, too, but lacking a sense of humour, all the same.

How things had changed.

Oh, the man still loved God. Still practiced daily with his sword. Still maintained a certain level of self-mastery. But his harder edges had softened. Gabriel's love for Breanna had given him serenity that had not been there before. Or perhaps, Jacques mused, it had always been there. It simply needed the love of a woman to set it free.

Suppressing a sigh, he looked down at the missive in his hand. It had arrived that morning, addressed solely to him. He knew, before he'd even inspected the seal, who had sent it.

It had been dispatched nearly a month earlier from a remote location in the Languedoc region of southern France, not too far from the Basque lands of Jacques' birth. It had been written by a Templar priest who usually went by the name of Father Pierre Sabatier.

Usually.

Since the Templar arrestation the previous October, Jacques had often wondered what had become of the man. Now he knew. Some things never changed.

A shadow moved across his line of vision.

"Is it something you can share?" Ewan asked, with concern rather than intrusiveness.

"Gladly." Jacques handed him the missive. "If there are things I have not shared with you, Brother, 'tis only because you've never asked me about them."

Ewan remained silent for a while as he read, heaving a soft sigh as he handed the missive back. "Are you going?"

Jacques gave him a derisive look. "What do you think?"

"This priest doesn't say what he wants from you. It might be a trap."

"I'm flattered you think someone would go to all that trouble just to entice me back to France." Jacques shook his head. "Pierre Sabatier is no ordinary priest, Ewan. He's one of several men who are the eyes and ears of the Templar order. I've worked with him before."

"When are you leaving?"

"In a day or two."

"That soon?" Ewan drew a breath. "Will you be coming back?"

"God willing, Ewan," Jacques replied. "God willing."

To be continued…

Thank you so much for reading The Sword and the Spirit, 'Gabriel'. If you have enjoyed the book, please consider sharing your reading pleasure with others by leaving a review on Amazon or Goodreads, or both!

Notes: **Baron Robert de Clifford,** Warden of the Marches and Marshal of England. This character, while used fictionally in this story, is a real historical figure. Robert de Clifford (c.1274 – 1314) had extensive estates in the historic counties of Cumberland, Westmorland and Yorkshire. In August of 1308, he was also appointed captain and chief guardian of Scotland under Edward II. He was killed by the Scots at the battle of Bannockburn in 1314 and is buried at Shap Abbey in Cumbria.

St Bega is also taken from history. She is purported to have come from Ireland and landed at **St Bees,** which does lie on the west Cumbrian (previously Cumberland) coast.

Made in the USA
Middletown, DE
12 September 2023

38089655R10156